# The Copperfield House

Katie Winters

# Chapter One

October 17, 1996

It was the night before everything at The Copperfield House changed forever.

Julia would remember it for the rest of her life.

The Copperfield House, located between Dionis Beach and Jettis Beach on the northern coastline of Nantucket Island, was a feast for the senses. The old Victorian home was built in 1877. It was purchased by the Copperfields in 1974, right after their return from Paris, directly before the birth of their first child.

Over the next few years, Bernard and Greta Copperfield filled the home with promise, love, and the glorious aroma of Greta's French cooking. They were often seen walking along the waterline as the waves frothed toward them, catching the last of the afternoon light.

It was a dream of a place. Maybe it was too good to be true.

"Let's fill it with art, writing, children, music, and stories,"

Greta had told Bernard early on, which had led them to establish The Copperfield House as an artist residency. Slowly but surely, artists from all fields and backgrounds filled the rooms of one-half of The Copperfield House, where they thrived in the creative environment that Nantucket Island offered, swapping stories at the dinner table and speaking intellectually with Bernard and Greta.

A filmmaker who'd spent time at The Copperfield House in the late eighties had made a documentary about the old house. He'd interview artists and writers who'd spent time there, illustrating the space as a "haven for creatives in a world of money-money-money."

The other half of The Copperfield House was reserved only for the Copperfield family— where Bernard and Greta could nurture their children, dipping in and out of the creative world as they pleased. Greta had never thought of herself only as just an "artist" or just a "mother." Her heart told her she could play both roles and do them well.

Bernard Copperfield was something of a revolutionary writer. He was renowned for his one-thousand-page masterpiece, a novel set in the future that was said to be a work of genius. Greta was a worthy writer in her own right, having published several short story collections and poems with an east-coast publisher. Bernard frequently cited Greta as his "greatest companion" and "a much better writer than me." Greta loved him with a pure, honest, and true heart.

In October 1996, the Copperfields' third child, Julia Copperfield, was only seventeen years old, a long-legged, whip-smart teenager with a propensity for daydreaming, growing lost in the chaos of a summer's day, and running around with her boyfriend, Charlie Bellows. Her older brother, Quentin, was living out in Los Angeles, trying out a career as an actor, while her older sister Alana, was in New York City, modeling for small-time agencies and trying to make it big. The youngest daughter, Ella, was a bit of a mystery, but Ella liked it that way.

They were the gifted Copperfield children—the Copperfields who had it all.

* * *

On this last night before everything changed forever, Charlie Bellows dropped Julia Copperfield off at The Copperfield House at thirty minutes past five. His dark chocolate eyes were only slits as he took in the full picture of Julia, who wore his big leather jacket and a little red dress and a pair of tights with holes in the knees.

"What's that look for?" Julia asked him, her throat tightening.

Charlie shrugged, dropped a hand over the small of her back, and whispered in her ear so that the tiny hairs on the back of her neck stood straight up.

"You've got to be the prettiest girl I've ever seen in my life," he told her.

Had Julia been older than seventeen, perhaps she'd have rolled her eyes at such a cheesy statement. But here and now, she took in the brevity of his words, closed her eyes, and kissed him deeply, her arms slung across his shoulders as the autumn wind howled around them.

Behind her, the front door of The Copperfield House screamed open. Julia and Charlie's kiss broke as her older and only brother, Quentin, called out his greeting.

"Hey! Are you ever going to come inside to welcome your brother home?"

Julia cackled excitedly. She leaped forward, her jet-black hair in a stream behind her as she rushed toward Quentin, who was five years older than her and back for a visit from LA.

"There he is! Quentin Copperfield, the famous actor!" she cried.

Quentin had all the looks of an up-and-coming actor. His cheekbones were jagged, his jaw chiseled, his dark hair shaggy and fit for a hero. He was six-foot-three, just like their father, and his voice was deep and powerful, the kind of thing you wanted to hold onto as assurance during dark times.

Julia hugged him, then took stock of him, his California tan and large cartoonish-looking muscles. According to Alana, Julia's elder sister, Quentin's Los Angeles life outside of auditioning was a lot of hours at the gym and guzzling green smoothies. Apparently, this was what all the actors drank on their quest for beautiful skin, gorgeous hair, and cinched waistlines.

"Is that Julia?" Suddenly, Alana stepped out from the foyer, a knock-out beauty queen who stood five-foot-nine, with shocking green eyes and a moody pout.

"Oh my gosh!" Julia flung herself into her older sister's arms, shivering with excitement. "I had no idea you both would be here tonight."

"We decided to surprise Bernard and Greta," Quintin said.

"Since when are you calling Mom and Dad by their real names?" Alana asked, her smile crooked.

"Is New York City giving you an attitude these days?" Quintin asked her. "You know what LA people think of NYC people..."

Alana stuck out her tongue. With her face scrunched and her tongue flailing, she looked a lot more like the sister Julia remembered from their Nantucket days than the swanky model working her way up the food chain in the United States' most cutthroat city.

"You coming in, Charles?" Alana called over Julia's head teasingly. "Mom's made yet another feast."

Julia twisted around to spot Charlie, gangly and still tan

from the summertime, his dark blonde hair scraggly from the strong autumn winds. He hated being called Charles. Everyone knew that. Her heart surged with love for him.

"Come on, Charles!" Quentin called.

"I gotta get back home," Charlie returned, drawing his thumb back behind him to point in the direction of his place. "But Julia, I'll pick you up for school tomorrow?"

"She'll be waiting for you!" Alana cooed playfully as she drew her arm over Julia's shoulder and tugged her in.

"Give her a break." Greta Copperfield stood in the foyer with a spatula lifted in the air and a gorgeous smile plastered from ear to ear. "Nobody teased you about your high school boyfriends, Alana."

"That's such a lie. Quentin always made fun of me," Alana shot back.

"Not that you could stick to any one boyfriend for long," Quentin teased. "You made those high school boys crazy."

"And then you abandoned them for that hot-shot artist," Julia jumped in, finding her voice with her older siblings.

Alana's cheeks burned red. She raised a hand, ruffling her textured hair with outstretched fingers.

"How is our Asher these days?" Greta asked, tilting her head. "He was one of the most promising painters The Copperfield House had ever seen."

"I tried to get him to come back with me," Alana explained timidly. "But it's difficult to tear him from his work."

"Once an artist finds their flow, it's important to stay there." Bernard Copperfield spoke this wisdom from the circular staircase just right of the foyer, where he stood in a tweed suit, his hands pressed against his hips as he surveyed his wife and three of his four children.

Alana, Quentin, Julia, and Greta beamed up at him, the renowned novelist, the sturdy father, the loyal husband, the intellectual. They loved him to pieces. At forty-five years old, he'd retained his handsome looks yet lent them texture with salt-and-pepper curls, a salt-and-pepper beard, and a wardrobe that Greta described as *"professor on a liberal art campus."*

"Dad!" Alana rushed forward to hug him, closing her eyes as she bent her forehead against his shoulder.

"You should have told me you'd arrived," Bernard said.

"We didn't want to bother you," Quentin offered. "Mom says you're working on a brand-new project."

"When he finds the time, that is," Greta said. "The artists and writers in the residency always want to bend his ear."

"It's part of the reason they come to The Copperfield House in the first place," Bernard added with a shrug. "They want conversation and communion and guidance."

Alana, Quentin, Greta, Julia, and Bernard headed to the kitchen, where Greta continued to bustle around, preparing a French-inspired feast for the night ahead. There were a number of reasons to celebrate. First off, Quentin and Alana had returned home for the first time since they'd moved to the big cities on either coast. Secondly, one of the writers-in-residence, who'd resided at The Copperfield House since January of 1996, had just signed an agreement with a Los Angeles production company. She planned to move out west within the month to start work on her first film.

This particular writer-in-residence, Marcia Conrad, was a twenty-five-year-old Tufts University graduate with sun-kissed locks, luscious lips, skillfully-drawn eyeliner, and a sharp writer's voice. When Bernard had first accepted Marcia as a writer-in-residence, he'd told the rest of the Copperfields that he felt Marcia would *"really be something one day."*

As the Copperfields chatted and snacked in the kitchen, Marcia appeared in the doorway dressed in a black turtleneck and baggy blue jeans. She greeted the rest of the Copperfields warmly and then cried, "Greta! I told you not to go all-out for tonight's dinner."

"Come now, Marcia," Greta returned as she stirred through a large pot of potatoes au gratin. "You've worked hard the past ten months. Now that you're about to leave the nest, we have to send you off with a proper meal. We don't want you forgetting all about us once you jet off to Los Angeles."

"I told you to look me up when you get there," Quentin affirmed, a celery stick lifted toward his lips. "I can introduce you to some cool people. Los Angeles parties make you realize just how small Nantucket is."

Marcia blushed timidly. "I don't know if I have it in me to fit in with your cool Los Angeles types, Quentin."

"She's like me, Quentin," Bernard said good-naturedly. "More willing to stay inside with a good book on a Friday evening than stay out all night with strangers."

"You say that now," Greta returned. "But the Bernard Copperfield I met back in Paris in the seventies was more than willing to stay out all night and into the next morning, given the chance and enough cash in his pockets."

Bernard laughed, scrunching his eyes closed, so that little wrinkles inched toward his hairline. Greta stood on her tippy toes to plant a kiss on his cheek. Quentin, Alana, and Julia rolled their eyes instinctively. They'd always been privy to the enormous amount of love their parents still had for one another, even after all these years.

"Ah! Before I forget," Marcia said suddenly, rubbing her palms together mischievously. "Julia, remember that poem you showed me the other day?"

Julia's eyes widened with surprise as she cursed inwardly. *Hadn't she told Marcia she wanted to keep her writing to herself? Hadn't she told her that she wanted to keep her parents out of it for once?*

"A poem?" Bernard asked. His eyes widened, then moved toward his third child excitedly. "Julia, I thought you'd given up writing years ago."

7

"She hasn't," Marcia affirmed. "And she's so good, Bernard. Maybe even as good as you."

All eyes were suddenly upon Julia. Julia twirled the black strands of her hair into a tight coil around her finger. Marcia gave her a coaxing smile.

"I thought you could read for us tonight after dinner," Marcia continued. "I plan to do a little reading of my script, and a few of the other writers here at The Copperfield House have agreed to read portions of their works in progress. It would be a treat to have another generation of Copperfield writers read during my going-away party."

"Julia, you really should. You know that if you never share your work with the world, it's almost like it never existed," Bernard informed her, pushing his glasses back up the bridge of his nose.

"You're just nosy, Daddy," Alana told him playfully. "If Julia wants to keep her work to herself, that's her business."

"I'll do it," Julia offered suddenly, her voice quivering and unsure.

"Apparently, Julia's a Copperfield, after all..." Quentin teased. "The rest of us are so hungry for attention all the time."

"Don't tease your sister," Greta snapped a kitchen towel in Quentin's direction. "And get out to the dining room to set the table. There's thirteen of us for dinner tonight."

"Lucky number thirteen," Quentin groaned, tugging Alana to grab the fine china from the armoire. They would use their best set tonight.

Bernard leaned tenderly toward Julia, his brown eyes soft and coaxing. "Julia, why didn't you tell me that you were hard at work on your poetry again?"

Julia could have given her father fifteen different answers.

She could have told him she resented that everyone "expected" her to be a writer, artist, actor, or musician because she was a Copperfield.

She could have told him she'd felt she wasn't half as good as her genes should have allowed.

She could have told him she wasn't sure of herself or her voice or the direction her poems had taken her.

But instead, she shrugged and answered, "Don't you ever like to keep a secret? All for yourself?"

Bernard's smile was crooked and knowing. For years afterward, Julia remembered this smile, marveled at it and wondered if this was some sort of clue, proof that Bernard Copperfield, who was beloved across Nantucket Island, was really up to no good. But at this moment, Julia felt only her father's love— and drummed up the courage to recite her poem to the Copperfield family and the others at The Copperfield House. Perhaps this would be a crowning moment, proof that she wasn't half-bad at the whole poetry thing. Perhaps this would give her the confidence to keep going.

\* \* \*

When Greta wanted to demonstrate her love for Bernard, she'd pore over her old French recipe books to remind him of their lost days in Paris. Armed with her love and endless creativity, she cooked up mouth-watering and inventive French-inspired five-course meals, such as fig and goat cheese tarts, duck breasts with cherry sauce, smoked salmon canapes, and thick layered chocolate mousses or cheesecakes. In the artist residency pamphlets, The Copperfield House was cited for its numerous benefits for creativity, *"The lady of the house cooks fantastic French-inspired meals. I gained ten pounds in my three-month stay, but I don't regret a thing,"* one ex-resident had written.

That night was no different. Julia was overly-stuffed after course five, so much so that she stretched out her legs under the table, closed her eyes halfway, and fell into the sleepy haze of post-dinner. One of the musicians had a guitar positioned gently across his lap and strummed it delicately, gazing out the window at the gray haze of the early evening. Marcia sat alongside Bernard Copperfield, speaking about the nuances of one of the scenes in her recent manuscript. Alana bragged to Quentin about a party she and her boyfriend, Asher, had attended on the Upper West Side at an apartment that had sold for four million dollars. Julia hadn't a clue how anyone made money in their lives; she hadn't a clue how she would ever survive. What was life like outside The Copperfield House, anyway? This was all she'd ever known.

Ella, the youngest Copperfield, sat beside Julia, smearing her fork through her potatoes au gratin distractedly. She was the music-obsessed member of the family who had recently formed a band with a few other high school students. Julia had witnessed her all-out scream-singing at a recent garage concert, where her black fingernails had wrapped pointedly around a microphone as she'd howled out the lyrics.

"Are you okay?" Julia muttered to Ella, as she'd hardly heard her speak during dinner.

Ella shrugged flippantly. She was fifteen, volatile, and moody— far different than the rest of the Copperfields. She seemed to appreciate this about herself. She adored her difference. Sometimes, Julia was jealous of it. It was obvious what made Ella special. Julia, however, struggled with knowing what made her different.

Suddenly, Bernard stood with a wine glass extended, clearing his throat so that the other twelve members paused their conversation and turned their heads his way.

"Thank you. Thank you. I'd like to take this moment to congratulate one of our most faithful writers-in-residence, Marcia Conrad. Marcia, it's been such a pleasure watching you gain traction as a writer and an artist since your arrival at The Copperfield House in January. Now that you're off to Los Angeles to become everything you're meant to be, we celebrate you and all you've accomplished. We ask that you stop in for a meal, some conversation, and maybe a glass of wine or two, when you find the time."

Marcia pressed a kiss against her hand and blew it toward Bernard. Off to the right of Marcia, one of the musicians whispered into a filmmaker's ear. The filmmaker giggled menacingly. Julia's stomach twisted. *What were they laughing about? Did they think there was something strange about Marcia and Bernard's relationship?*

Julia blinked down toward her mother, who'd witnessed the blown kiss but seemed unfazed. Greta and Bernard Copperfield had the sort of marriage you didn't question. Probably, Marcia was just endlessly grateful for Bernard, this father figure of sorts. Besides, Bernard Copperfield was also something of a genius and certainly regarded as one of the top minds on the eastern seaboard.

This was another reason Julia struggled to show him any of her work. He was a genius. He'd probably pick her apart.

"I suppose it's time for me to speak," Marcia said, her voice flowing slowly yet sweet like honey. She stood, adjusting the black turtleneck to highlight the slender cut of her waist. "My time here at The Copperfield House has been genuinely life-changing. I've spent endless hours walking up and down the beaches and gazing out across the waters. I've had ups and downs and in-betweens and really come into my own with my creative work. Bernard, you've been such a Godsend, pushing my creative impulses in so many new directions. And you've introduced me to some of the greatest minds I've ever encountered, men and women on this island who read, write, and theorize far more than anyone I met in a university setting."

Marcia continued, seeming a tad tipsy and enamored, until suddenly, she flashed an arm out toward Julia and announced, "I've recently had a little moment of mentorship myself. I sat down with Julia and chatted to her about her recent poetry collection, which, I have to say, bleeds talent. What luck, isn't it? To be born into The Copperfield House. Every day must have been like a writer's residency. Every day must have felt wild with imagination."

The others at the table turned their formidable gazes toward Julia. She swallowed the lump in her throat as she gathered her notebook to her chest. Family pressure was something else. Her knees clacked together nervously as she stood to wade her way toward the head of the table.

"Remember, everyone. The young woman you're about to hear is only seventeen years old," Marcia continued. "Seventeen years old, with a wealth of emotion and a promising future ahead of her. Where was it you said you wanted to apply to for college, Julia?"

"Um." Julia's heart beat as swiftly as a rabbit's. "Potentially, Yale."

"Yale?" Bernard sounded breathless with excitement. "Julia... Why didn't you tell us?"

"She also mentioned Princeton and Tufts," Marcia added proudly.

"You should check out Oberlin," one of the musicians offered.

"I'll um. I'll look into it." Julia now stood at the head of the table. She flashed a hand across the haze of dark hair across her shoulder. *What was her poem about again? She could hardly remember it.*

"Are you ready, Julia?" Marcia asked coaxingly.

"Come on, Julia. It's like they tell me when I'm modeling. If you don't believe in yourself, who else will?" Alana spouted.

"Wow. Sage advice, Alana," Quentin quipped sarcastically.

"Shut up," Alana shot back.

"Could the elder siblings please quiet down?" Bernard

asked somberly. "My daughter would like to share her art with us. And I, for one, would like to hear it."

Finally, silence fell around them as Julia scrambled through her notebook, searching for the poem she'd shared with Marcia. When she finally found it, there was a strange high-pitched noise in her ears, proof she was in over her head.

"This is a poem I called 'We Are Who We Are,'" Julie breathed, her voice wavering even as she forced her way into it.

We are who we are,
Birthed, cradled, comforted
Toys strewn across beaches and
My mother's soft voice as
She whispers it's time to go
Inside, hide away from the beating
Heart of sunshine, a heat so
Colossal, it seems to echo.
The Copperfield House, our
Home so glorious it deserves its own
name, folds its great arms
Over us, protects us.
There, we are who we are,
The Copperfields
our doors open
to the promise of
Others' creativity, and our
Hope for the future powerful
Enough to charge us toward
The future. It's just beginning.

The Copperfields and the artists-in-residence burst to their feet, their applause swelling through the air. Julia, who'd witnessed countless other writers read their work like this, nearly collapsed with glory.

Bernard Copperfield's eyes glowed with tears of recognition at the far end of the table. As the applause eased back to silence, he came toward her side of the room to swallow her up in a hug.

"I'm so proud of you, Julia. You are a Copperfield, through and through. I love you to pieces. And your art is proof that your heart feels the gravity of the universe."

# Chapter Two

Why was October 17, 1996, the last day before everything changed forever?

Why couldn't this cozy and creative ecosystem at The Copperfield House go on for many more years?

It all began with a daring accusation.

On October 18, 1996, five of Bernard Copperfield's dearest friends announced that he'd separately swindled them, ultimately stealing upward of eighteen million dollars. Naturally, as Bernard Copperfield had been a beloved and honorable member of Nantucket Island for decades, the accusations were alarming. Still, why would all five of Bernard Copperfield's best friends point to Bernard if they didn't have proof? Why would they purposefully drag his name through the dirt, a man they'd previously dined with, drank with, and traveled with? A man they'd previously loved?

In the wake of this accusation, several local businesses announced that they believed Bernard was the reason behind a considerable loss of their funds. The evidence against him began to mount. And by the end of October 19<sup>th</sup>, Bernard Copperfield was taken from The Copperfield House and put into custody.

Julia witnessed the arrest.

In fact, she and Ella stood quivering in the corner of The Copperfield House living room, behind the baby grand piano, as the police read Bernard his rights and then ushered him out and into their police cruiser. He looked ridiculous in his tweed professor suit, his little round glasses sat on the bridge of his nose as the police wrapped the handcuffs around his wrists. Julia pinched the bottom of her stomach in an attempt to wake up from this nightmare. Her eyes remained glued to this current reality. *Perhaps this was really her life.*

After they took Bernard to the downtown jail, The Copperfield House cleared out rather quickly. The artists, writers, musicians, and filmmakers packed up their backpacks and fled the island on the next ferry, most without honoring the payment agreements of their residencies. Quentin and Alana high-tailed it back to Los Angeles and New York City. They hardly hugged anyone goodbye.

This left Greta, Ella, and Julia alone in the Victorian house, which seemed to creak with loneliness in the wake of the accusations. The heart of their home had been destroyed, tainted.

The first night after Bernard was taken, Greta didn't bother to cook. Ella and Julia boiled a pot of pasta on the stovetop and listened for some sign of movement from their mother upstairs, where she remained in the bedroom she shared with Bernard. They slid pesto sauce across the noodles and ate gingerly, both conscious of how useless it felt to eat when it seemed the world wouldn't go forward another day.

"Do you think he really did it?" Ella asked her, a big hunk of noodles wrapped around her fork.

Julia's throat tightened. She remembered the hug her father had given her after she'd read her poem only a couple of nights before, his whispered words that her heart felt the gravity of the universe. What did those words mean if, in actuality, her father was a swindling thief and a liar?

"I don't know," Julia told her simply.

Ella dropped her forkful of noodles. "It doesn't make any sense."

"Maybe they've made some kind of mistake," Julia tried.

A beetle inched its way across the corner of the kitchen. Julia yelped and jumped from her chair, which fell back and rattled against the floor. Ella just sat there, unbothered. The majority of the time, The Copperfield House was spotless and glowing, proof of their mother's words that a *"tidy house meant a tidy mind."* This beetle seemed evidence that the Copperfield mindset wasn't so tidy just then.

"It must be a mistake," Julia answered herself timidly. "I mean, it's Dad. Why would Dad do something like that?"

Ella shrugged, still unable to meet Julia's eyes. "People do all sorts of things, don't they?"

The winter was nearly unbearable. Julia, who'd never had many friends anyway, stuck as close to Charlie as she could, trying to guard herself against the endless barrage of insults about her father, her family, and herself.

Ella, too, kept to herself and threw all her energy into her band. She practiced for hours on end, fine-tuning her guitar and piano skills and writing songs late into the night. When her teacher tried to contact Greta about Ella sleeping through class, Greta didn't bother answering the phone. At a loss, the teacher continued to let Ella sleep. It was a delicate situation, after all. Nobody knew quite what to think of it.

After the trial began, things went from nearly unbearable to absolutely heinous.

The trial played out on Nantucket Island itself, where Bernard's nearest and dearest friends could sit on the stand and explain the horrors that Bernard Copperfield had put them through.

"We trusted him. He was one of our best friends. And he lied and cheated us out of millions of dollars."

"Why do you think he did it?" the lawyer asked, feigning shock. Lawyers were nothing if not actors who'd learned a few more rules.

"I genuinely have no idea. I thought The Copperfield House was doing just fine on its own. And he was a top-selling author. It genuinely makes no sense to me," one of his friends, Gregory Puck, said on the stand. "I never imagined I'd hate Bernard Copperfield. But when I learned what he did to myself and several of our friends, I found myself with genuine feelings of hatred. I don't know what to do with all of my memories with him by my side."

When Julia heard him say that, she wanted to laugh.

After all, what did he care? He was Gregory Puck, a millionaire in his own right, with a number of other friends by his side.

With these accusations, Julia Copperfield had lost so much more.

She'd lost her father.

She'd lost her high opinion of him.

She'd lost her belief that her mother and father had the perfect marriage.

And that only mounted a little later in the trial, when several of Bernard's friends mentioned "*Marcia Conrad.*"

"She was always hanging around with him," Gregory continued. "Always at his beck and call. Always made it very clear to the rest of us that... Well..."

"Can you please continue with your statement?" the lawyer pushed.

"I care deeply for Greta Copperfield," Gregory stated. "She is a dear friend of mine."

"Please, continue your statement," the lawyer countered.

"I don't mean to be crass, but it seemed to me and the rest of my colleagues and friends that Bernard Copperfield had entered into a sexual relationship with Marcia Conrad. We now assume that he wanted to put this money aside to start a new life with her."

During this testimony, Julia sat beside Greta Copperfield, her proud and gorgeous mother— a woman who'd mastered the French language and French cooking all in a single year. Perhaps a different woman would have crumpled during this testimony, there in the midst of over a hundred people who watched her knowingly.

But Greta Copperfield was a lady.

And ladies waited to crumple in the privacy of their home.

Greta remained in her bedroom for the better part of the next few weeks. Ella and Julia took turns bringing her water and food, things that were relatively easy to eat, like crackers and cheese and soups. All the while, Greta stared through the blue haze from the light of the television, not even seeming to watch the various series or movies she'd put on. Neither Julia nor Ella had ever seen their mother like this.

Alana and Quintin didn't call home very much. It seemed they both wanted to distance themselves from the entire scandal as much as possible. Quentin was considering changing his last name, as he didn't want to be associated with their father. Alana spoke about marrying Asher, the painter, to solve that issue and create a "new era" for herself. Neither of them seemed to care about the teenage girls left at home.

As Ella turned more inward, communicating almost exclusively through lyrics with her band, Julia found herself alone in the world— with only Charlie by her side.

Charlie. Charlie Bellows.

19

Julia and Charlie.

The magical teenage couple that everyone had adored, for summer after summer.

It seemed that their magic had dissipated. There were no more free milkshakes, no more eager greetings. More and more, Julia insisted that Charlie come to The Copperfield House and hide out in her bedroom, usually with junk food and VHS tapes. They cuddled under her blankets, nibbling at the edge of Twizzlers and watching David Lynch movies.

Once, Charlie asked Julia, "Have you written any poetry lately?"

At this, Julia scoffed, "I can barely get myself through the day. I'm officially retired from poetry and writing. Forever."

Around this same time, Charlie asked her another question that felt sharper and more difficult to answer.

"Do you think your father had an affair with that writer? Marcia?"

Julia groaned inwardly and pressed her hands over her eyes. There had been signs, hadn't there? Perhaps she'd been too naive to understand them. Perhaps her belief that her father's good character was unquestionable had blinded her.

"I don't know. He probably did, right?" Julia finally tried, her voice wavering. "I mean, if he did everything else, he probably did that, too? Right?"

Charlie was quiet after that. He bundled himself around her, pressing play on the remote control. They flowed easily into another strange Lynchian universe, finally forgetting their own reality, at least for a little while.

* * *

Bernard Copperfield was given twenty-five years in prison for his crimes.

The sentencing was carried out about two months before

Julia Copperfield was slated to graduate from high school, on April 12th, 1997.

But as she watched her father in the courthouse that afternoon, something in her gut told her she couldn't stick around for what happened next. She felt rotted out. People's eyes followed her, distrusting. Nantucket was no longer her home. And soon, she felt sure that The Copperfield House would erode against the powerful Atlantic elements.

Back at The Copperfield House, Julia and Charlie sat at the edge of her bed and listened to Greta down the hall as she wailed with sorrow. To Julia, it was the most painful sound in the world, other than listening to someone die. Perhaps in a way, a part of Greta really was dying. *What did it mean to continue living when so much of what you'd built your life on was a lie?*

"I think we should go." Julia stared directly toward the wall, her eyes glazed.

"Yeah. Let's go get something to eat or go for a walk," Charlie told her. "We should get out of the house. The air is poisonous in here."

Julia let nearly a full minute of silence pass before she spoke again.

"That's not really what I mean."

"Okay... What do you mean?" Charlie's large puppy-dog eyes nearly shattered her heart.

Julia dropped back on the bed so that it bounced around beneath her. Charlie followed her lead and drew his fingers through hers. There was a crack up her bedroom ceiling, proof enough that the house was falling apart in more ways than one.

"I want to leave Nantucket. Right now."

"Julia... Come on. It's April. We're about to graduate from high school."

"It's awful, Charlie. I think if I stay in this house for another second, I'll suffocate."

"I could ask my parents if you could come live with us. It's not like they don't know about us, and it's not like they don't know we will get married someday."

Julia propped herself up on her elbow. Her love for Charlie seemed like the only thing she knew how to cling to during the violence of this storm.

"I love you, Charlie."

"I love you, too, Julia."

"I can't stay here. I can't stay in Nantucket. Do you understand me?"

Charlie's eyes twinkled with the light from the hanging bulb. He took a deep breath so that his stomach rose and fell. He then linked his fingers with hers, drawing her hand over his chest, right over the bursting beat of his heart.

"We don't need anyone else, Charlie. We don't need my family or your family or any other person on Nantucket Island. We don't need some stupid high school diploma. What does it mean, anyway? We've read more books than anyone at that high school put together. We have better intellectual discussions than our teachers ever possibly could. We've learned all we can at that school. And we've done all we can on this stupid island. Won't you come with me, Charlie? Won't you dream up a life with me? I need you, Charlie. It's just you and me. Forever."

# Chapter Three

April 2022

Five-inch heels. *Great idea, Julia.* Today, of all days, one of the most torrentially rainy days of early April in Chicago, heels had been a brilliant idea.

Her heels skidded across the pavement as she hustled down the crosswalk. Her umbrella was positioned strategically, a little crooked so not to snarl the hair of the older woman beside her. That woman wore tennis shoes rather than heels, a sensible choice. *But did that woman own her own publishing house on the forty-first floor of Willis Tower?* Probably not.

Julia had learned a long time ago, during the early days of opening her own publishing house, that the world demanded far more of you as a woman. It demanded you be five minutes early, over-prepared, slightly underfed, always overworked, all while standing in five-inch heels. Even now, given the supposed "equality" of the times, she sensed judgment from all sides of all aisles. Women had to be better. Period.

Julia burst into the foyer of the Willis Tower, collapsing her umbrella swiftly and greeting the security guards with a half-smile. When they didn't return it, she brushed hers away evenly. Her over-eager smiles were left-over from her Nantucket days, back when islanders had greeted one another happily. It had all been sunshine, ice cream cones and big, beautiful waves until it hadn't been any more.

Julia rushed into the next elevator, locking eyes with another businessman who was headed to the twenty-fifth floor. He grunted hello, dropping his gaze. Julia's stomach curdled with embarrassment.

*Did everyone know what trouble she was in?*

*Was she delusional to think she could dig her way out of this one?*

"How are you doing, Bob?" she asked him, alone in the elevator as it whizzed upward.

"Can't complain." He gave her zero follow-up questions. Clearly, he thought of her as rotten meat.

She didn't blame him.

Fifteen years ago, Julia had officially begun Orchard Publishing with just three employees and a single office in Logan's Square, which hadn't even been a hip part of Chicago at the time. Fresh off several best-selling hits, Julia had moved her publishing company to Willis Tower in mid-2013, where they'd enjoyed approximately four years of moderate success.

What she and her colleagues called "the big misses" began in 2018. They'd thrown most of their eggs in the metaphorical baskets of books that had generated only forty percent of the suspected income. Other writers they'd banked on had gotten into inappropriate social media disputes with their readers, which had resulted in an immense backlash against the books themselves.

Although Julia was officially the owner of the company, she had received some backlash, as she'd championed a male writer who'd written a book that included a scene of domestic abuse against a woman. It should have gone without saying that Julia was anti-domestic abuse. *Wasn't that obvious?* The scene had been essential to get a sense of the dynamic between the two main characters, both of whom had come from toxic upbringings. Also, not all books were meant to be "easy reading," were they? That said, many readers and non-readers alike had decided to demonize Julia and the writer in question, which had resulted in an even steeper decline in book sales.

Now, in the wake of the first quarter of the year, Julia and Orchard Publishing found themselves at a loss. What kind of business owner let her entire company fall into such disrepair?

Julia arrived at her nine-thirty appointment at nine-twenty-four sharp. She removed her laptop from her bag, opened it, and clicked at her pen anxiously until her accountant, Randy, stepped through the door. Randy was a damp mess. His hair caked across his forehead; the bottoms of his slacks were sopping.

If Julia had ever gone through the rain ill-prepared, she'd never have managed to open up her own publishing house in the first place. Probably, her husband would have had her committed. Her children would have never spoken her name again.

"Hi, Randy," Julia greeted brightly, wanting to believe that everything could be all right again. *Fake it till you make it, right?*

"Julia." Randy's tone seemed less-than-optimistic. He splayed a large folder across the table and collapsed in the chair across from her. "I was up all night going over the numbers. Crunching everything I could."

"Everything you could?" Julia had her doubts about that.

"There have been too many hits to the brand," Randy continued. "As you can see, your revenue was already on a steady decline until last autumn's Twitter war."

Randy lifted a print-out from his folder and gestured

toward the sharp drop, which had been in October, before the smallest of inclines in December for Christmas gifts.

"I guess consumers don't check Twitter before Christmas," Julia tried to joke.

"The thing is, Julia. Many of them do."

Julia's stomach clenched so tightly that she thought she might have to run to the bathroom and vomit up her morning coffee. Her lips curved downward as she muttered, "So what's the damage, Randy? What can we do next?"

"I've said this before, but I'll say it again— and it's the last time, Julia. You're running on fumes. You need to fire most of your staff and leave Willis Tower immediately. The ship is going down. And if you want to keep Orchard Publishing around, you need to high-tail it back to that little office space in Logan's Square. Back where you came from."

Silence swelled around them. Julia cleared her throat, trying to find a single articulate thought within her anxious, swirling mind.

"You know that Logan's Square rents have quadrupled since 2012," she pointed out. Obviously, this wasn't the point.

"Decide which employees you want to keep. I have a list of prospective sub-leasers willing to take over the lease here in Willis Tower as soon as this week. This will keep you above water a little while longer."

Randy positioned the list of up-and-coming "rockstar companies" who eyed Orchard Publishing's place in Willis Tower with expectation and excitement. Obviously, these offices would project their revenue into the stars above. Julia had thought that, too.

"What are these companies?" Julia demanded as she read the list.

"The first two are yoga and smoothie start-ups," Randy explained. "Hair-Away is a social media firm meant to give confidence back to men who are losing their hair. You laugh, but it's extremely profitable. They're changing the narrative."

Julia's nostrils flared as anger flowed through her. "You're telling me that we've reached a state, as a country, where publishing houses that publish real books about ideas, thoughts, and emotions cannot make it— but a social media firm for men's hair loss can continue to profit?"

"They're not just profiting, Julia," Randy told her. "They're on the Fortune 500 list this year."

Julia kicked off her heels so that they clattered on the ground. Randy peeked under the table to see what she'd done.

With Julia's eyes to the corner, she whispered, "I gave everything to this company. I went days without sleeping. Worked tirelessly as a wife and a mother, unwilling to compromise."

"You should look into therapy," Randy told her simply as he returned his print-outs to his folder. "My brother-in-law lost his job last year and was in a bad state. But then, he started therapy, made time for fishing, and started a successful social media account about the meditation benefits of being on a boat all day."

Julia wondered what would happen to her company's profits if she was arrested for smacking her accountant across the face. Was that what business owners did? Would feminist social media channels say *"yes, queen!"* and hail her as the future of the industry?

Julia was lost in her thoughts for the remainder of the day. She felt like a puppet, with someone else operating the strings on high as she pushed herself through the tasks. First, she fired her secretary; then, she fired all but two of her editors; then, she cleared out all but one of her advertisers before making her way through the unpaid interns, who seemed relieved to learn that they'd still get "credit" for their time there but no longer had to come in. Julia then gathered the two editors and one marketer she'd kept around and explained she still wanted to keep Orchard Publishing running and had (barely) enough funds to continue paying them throughout the year.

"But we'll operate everything remotely," she explained simply, grateful that her voice didn't waver. "I'll throw myself into this work three times as hard as ever. I'll find the next brilliant writer. I'll read queries, speak with agents, and edit manuscripts till I'm spinning. Orchard Publishing won't go down without a fight."

The hang-dog faces of the remaining Orchard Publishing staff members weren't exactly inspiring. Julia watched them leave together like a pack of hungry dogs. Probably, they were headed to the nearest bar for several pints, where they could whisper about jobs in publishing they could get elsewhere, hopeful of getting out of Orchard Publishing as soon as possible.

# Chapter Four

Just as she'd done for the previous twenty years, Julia took the train back from the city of Chicago to the suburb of Bartlett, where she and her husband had raised their three children. Bartlett was a cozy little town where everyone knew one another. All the houses had been built about twenty-five years ago to account for the young couples leaving the city to start their families, and entire "pedestrian" areas had been built up to create a sort of "city-living" feel, which was sterile but still okay. The train ride was a little more than an hour, which gave Julia time to fall into the beautiful haze of her favorite album, *Blue* by Joni Mitchell.

The album had always reminded her of her mother, Greta. She'd played the album on repeat during cloudy summer days as the Copperfields had sat around the house, reading books, writing in journals, or making little sketches. Julia's heart swelled with longing for those long-lost afternoons.

*Did Greta still listen to Joni Mitchell?*

*Did Greta still think of Julia at all?*

The three-bedroom cookie-cutter house on the western end

of Sumter Drive featured a basketball hoop in the front drive, a large dying bush that needed to be pulled out of the earth, and flower beds that would need plenty of tender-loving-care that spring. Julia stood before it, inspecting its beige coloring, its big plastic garage door, and the oil stain in the driveway, which had dripped out from her eldest's car before she'd moved out west and sold it.

This wasn't the first time Julia had compared her adult home to her childhood one.

In truth, The Copperfield House probably looked a lot different in memory than in reality. The Victorian home loomed heavy in Julia's mind, with its glorious artistic detail, enormous windows, hardwood floors, and flourishing curtains, which took on the Atlantic breezes.

Such a sharp contrast to this Midwestern house in the suburbs.

Such a sharp contrast to Julia's reality.

Julia pressed the garage door code into the side of the door and watched as the door began to raise toward the roof. The garage held only her vehicle, a shiny black SUV that she'd hardly driven since her last child had gone to university the previous autumn.

Her husband's car, a trendy Camaro, was, as usual, someplace else.

Julia kicked off her heels and paced toward the refrigerator, where she leafed out a bottle of rosé and poured herself half a glass. The kitchen was spotless, all the dishes put away, the coffee pot gleaming even after its morning use, and all the breakfast crumbs deposited in the silver trashcan. The refrigerator featured several family photographs, moments in time when her children had celebrated various life events, such as birthdays, graduations, and piano recitals.

Anna. Henry. Rachel. Her babies.

Seeing their faces made Julia's heart surge with love.

But seeing their faces also reminded Julia that she'd failed them.

She'd meant to be a powerful mother, a successful business-woman in her own right. Someone her children could respect and look up to.

Her phone dinged with a voice message from her husband. Julia took a long sip of her wine, coating her tongue with the dry, crisp liquid. She then pressed PLAY.

Jackson Crawford's voice bellowed through the speaker, strong and sure of itself.

*"Hey, babe. Chasing down a story tonight in Hyde Park. Don't wait up for me."*

Julia's nostrils flared. She resented voice messages. It was like their sender didn't have the "time" to type out a simple message. She refused to send a voice message back and instead texted.

**JULIA: Good luck tonight.**

**JULIA: Make sure you're home tomorrow.**

**JULIA: Remember. The kids are in town.**

Perhaps only to add to her irritation, Jackson sent a voice message back.

*"I know the kids are in town tomorrow. I wouldn't forget something like that."*

Julia rolled her eyes into her head, smacked her phone back on the counter, and made her way around the island, her wine glass in hand. Seconds later, she collapsed across the beige comfort of the couch, the remote control extended. In previous years, she'd prided herself on staying busy after work, going over manuscripts for the publishing house, helping one of her children with their homework, or assisting Rachel with her piano studies.

Now, she flicked through channels aimlessly as though she was on a mission to waste time.

Julia's husband, Jackson Crawford, was a renowned video

and print journalist. He'd had his own political and socioeco-
nomic column in his twenties and thirties, which had bolstered
him in the public eye. He'd finished his column in his late thirties and moved on to become a more public face, which was
proof, to Julia at least, that men's careers flourished as they aged
while women's floundered. Probably this wasn't entirely fair to
say, given that her publishing house's failure had nothing to do
with her age of forty-two. However, when she felt most
resentful of her husband, she paraded through these thoughts
angrily, usually while drinking wine.

Julia reached for her phone to text one of her children.
Rachel. She was the youngest, only nineteen, and had recently
left the nest. She went to college in Ann Arbor, Michigan, where
she majored in English Literature and minored in French.

**JULIA: Hi, honey. How was your French test
this morning?**

It took Rachel a little while to respond to her message. She
was probably studying in the library or grabbing coffee with a
cute boy, or eating lunch in the dining hall, whatever it was
nineteen-year-olds did during their first year of university. Julia
could only fantasize, as she'd taken a very different path in life.

**RACHEL: Hey, Mom. I think I messed up some
of the grammar. Thank God, it wasn't worth that
much of our grade.**

**RACHEL: Excited to see you tomorrow! Going
to bed early, so I don't miss the bus.**

**JULIA: You'd better not miss it! Your father and
I can't wait to see you.**

Julia continued to flick through the channels, never
lingering on any one show or news segment for longer than a
few minutes. She refilled her glass of wine soon after, half-
considering the concept of dinner before shoving the thought

away. Tonight was meant for digging into the depths of her despair. She undressed in the living room and splayed out in her underwear, something she'd seen Jackson do time and time again. It was just as much her house as it was his.

Jackson. Jackson Crawford.

Julia drew her nails across her stomach, gazing at the photograph of herself and Jackson perched on the fireplace mantel to the left of the television. The photo had been taken ten years ago when Julia had been thirty-two. Orchard Publishing had been on the up-and-up, and Julia had been the more "promising" professional in their couple-dom. Jackson had called her his "more powerful partner." At the time, he hadn't even resented it.

Back then, they'd had the children to consider. Anna had been twelve; Henry had been ten; Rachel had been nine. Personal resentments within their marriage had been more easily wiped away.

*Had she loved him back then? Really loved him?*

Julia leaped up to inspect the photograph closer. In it, thirty-two-year-old Julia had splayed a hand tenderly across Jackson's chest. Her eyes twinkled knowingly; Jackson played with the curls of her soft dark hair. They were certainly the portrait of a happy couple.

But to Julia, there in the shadows of her living room, she and Jackson looked like strangers.

Julia returned the photograph to the mantel and collapsed back on the couch. The room spun around her strangely as she continued to flick through the stations. Her thoughts were so rowdy, so loud as they tossed back and forth in her skull that she nearly missed the segment on Channel 4 that changed her life forever.

The headline was dramatic and jarring.

**NOVELIST     BERNARD     COPPERFIELD**

## RELEASED FROM PRISON AFTER SERVING A TWENTY-FIVE-YEAR SENTENCE.

Julia dropped the remote to the ground at her feet. On-screen, a female announcer, spoke:

"In the spring of 1997, Bernard Copperfield, renowned novelist and a man previously thought to be a genius, was sentenced to twenty-five years in prison for conning eighteen million dollars from friends, colleagues, and other wealthy residents that resided on Nantucket Island. Twenty-five years later, Copperfield has been released and is said to be returning to his home in Nantucket."

The station then showed an image that nearly shattered Julia's heart.

A man stepped out of a black vehicle in a sad-looking grey suit. The man was seventy with white-grey hair and wrinkles etched along his eyes, cheeks, neck, and a scowl. The man was hardly recognizable as Bernard Copperfield, save for his six-foot-three stature and something about his eyes. Julia leaped to her feet, gobsmacked by the sight of him.

She hadn't seen her father's face since April 12, 1997.

Yet there he was, in the flesh.

And he was headed back to Nantucket Island.

Back to The Copperfield House.

"What do you think you're going to find there?" Julia breathed, aghast. "Nobody is there for you. Nobody cares about you. Nobody wants you back."

"We can be sure that he's paid his debt to society," the newscaster continued confidently.

"Yes, to society. But what about his family?" Julia howled to the empty room.

Julia hadn't felt this enormous swell of rage in quite some time. During the years of profitability at her publishing house, she'd thought maybe she'd forgiven her father for his crimes, for destroying their family and tearing her life apart. *"It all worked out the way it was supposed to,"* she'd told Jackson once. *"I genuinely believe that."*

Julia grabbed her phone, feeling suddenly volatile. She had half a mind to call that newscaster on the air and tell her exactly what kind of hell Bernard Copperfield had created for the rest of the Copperfield family.

But it wasn't like the newscaster could understand.

No. The only people who could understand were the Copperfields themselves.

And she hadn't spoken to any of them since she'd left the island.

Well, that was kind of a lie.

She and Ella had had an email exchange a few years ago.

The email exchange had not gone well. Ella had told Julia to leave her alone.

Julia knew she was mostly to blame for Ella's less-than-stellar view of Julia. When Julia had taken off with Charlie only about two months before high school graduation, Ella was left in that big house alone with their depressed mother, who'd refused to get out of bed, let alone leave the house. Ella had felt abandoned. The others, Alana and Quentin, had stayed away for good, treating Nantucket like a plague den.

After Ella's graduation, she'd headed to NYC and begun the acclaimed indie rock band, Pottersville, with a drummer she'd met in Greenwich Village.

Since then, she and the drummer had had two children and a rocky relationship that was frequently written about in lesser-known indie rock tabloids. *"The on-again, off-again romance of indie rock band, Pottersville." "Who's caring for the kids?" "Is Ella Copperfield too old to be an indie rock musician?"* The tabloids were haunting. Julia had read each and every one religiously. She had alerts set up on her phone, which told her when anyone anywhere had written something about Ella. The fact that she'd recently learned her son, Henry, was a fan of

Pottersville had stopped her in her tracks, but she still hadn't told him Ella was his aunt. It would only complicate things.

She had alerts set up for Quentin and Alana, as well. But she resented Quentin's rise in popularity... and hardly ever saw anything about Alana unless it was about her husband, the acclaimed painter, Asher. In those articles, Alana was listed as little more than an afterthought. "His wife."

*Call one of them. Any of them.*

The thought rang out through Julia's mind. But it was laughable. What could she possibly say to her siblings about their father's release? They were all strangers, now.

"Good luck to you, Dad," she muttered to the television, her voice layered with sarcasm. "I'm sure Mom will be pleased to see you again."

# Chapter Five

"Happiness is a performance." The following afternoon, Julia quoted this to her reflection in the mirror, hands-on-hips as she investigated her athletic legs, wide-set shoulders, high Copperfield cheekbones, and swirling raven hair. She'd spent the previous forty-five minutes styling herself, drawing her eyeliner, and trying out different outfits. It was nearly time to pick up Rachel from the bus station and Anna from the airport. Henry, who went to the University of Chicago, would walk himself home from the train station, just as he always did.

By five o'clock that evening, the entirety of the Crawford clan would be under a single roof for the first time since the previous summer. Even at Christmas, Anna had stayed out in Seattle, choosing to double-down on the issue of the magazine she was interning for. It had nearly broken Julia's heart.

Rachel was second off the bus. She bounded down the steps, her hair wild and unkept, her smile electric. The driver helped her grab her backpack from the belly of the bus, which she swung over her shoulder before rushing toward Julia, her arms extended.

She looked healthy. She looked happy. She looked better than Julia ever could have hoped for.

"There she is!" Julia blinked back tears as she wrapped her arms around her youngest, her heart dropping into her stomach.

"Hi, Mom!" Rachel stepped back. "Cool outfit. I didn't know you had a leather jacket."

"I pulled it out of the back of the closet. It's from my younger days in Chicago with your father," Julia explained with a broad smile.

"Before you accidentally got pregnant with Anna and had to move to the burbs?" Rachel teased as she leaped into the front seat of the SUV, an action she'd performed countless times.

"You have to stop telling your older sister she was an accident," Julia groaned, feigning annoyance.

"That leather jacket screams 'single woman in the city,'" Rachel countered as Julia buckled her seatbelt and started the engine. "You wouldn't get away with wearing that thing in Bartlett."

"And yet, look at me, wearing 'that thing' in Bartlett." Julia teased, sticking out her tongue playfully.

As they drove out to Chicago's O'Hare Airport, Rachel chatted amicably about her recent weeks at the University of Michigan. She expressed her love-hate relationship with the French language, and her new lodging for next semester when she planned to live with two of her new best friends.

"You seem to really love the University of Michigan, honey," Julia stated as she eased the vehicle to a stop outside the airport.

"Are you surprised?" Rachel asked, turning to see her mother's facial expression.

"No. I knew when we visited it that it would be perfect for you," Julia told her. "I just wish it was closer to home, that's all."

"Hey, at least I'm not out in Seattle, like your accident child, Anna," Rachel countered.

"Oh my gosh! There she is!" As she hustled out from the automatic doors, Julia spotted her eldest, Anna, with a big backpack latched to her shoulders. At twenty-two, Anna Crawford looked powerful and fashion-forward, with sleek black jeans, a black turtleneck, and shiny black hair.

"My fashion icon!" Julia cried as she hugged her, inhaling a wave of perfume.

Anna giggled, clearly embarrassed but willing to shove the feeling aside. She knocked on the window next to Rachel's face, calling out, "Hey! Oldest gets to sit in front."

To this, Rachel just stuck out her tongue. Anna leaped in back, assembling her backpack beside her and crossing her ankles below. Julia noted that she wore flat boots, which were just as chic as any pair of five-inch heels she'd ever seen.

"Is Dad home?" Anna asked as they drove the rest of the way to their Bartlett suburban home. "He texted that he's been working crazy hours lately."

"Your father has been in demand. Chasing stories all over the city and appearing on talk shows...that kind of thing. He's even talked about writing a book about his experiences as a journalist," Julia told her daughters, waffling between pride and jealousy.

"Dad? Write a book?" Anna asked, incredulous.

Rachel snorted. Julia side-eyed her, curious.

"What was that for?" Julia asked.

"I don't know," Rachel offered. "It's just that, well..."

"Well, what?" Julia demanded.

"Dad's a brilliant journalist," Anna countered. "But I think what Rachel means is... There's no way Dad could write a whole book. He doesn't have the patience or the chops for it."

"You should ghostwrite it for him," Rachel quipped. "You're the writer in the family."

"Yeah, when will you take time off to write your book?" Anna asked brightly. "You always said that you'd commit to your art once Orchard Publishing could steer itself."

"One of these days," Julia heard herself lie through her teeth, cursing herself for ever having told her children about her innermost dreams. Those were better kept latched tight inside.

"Oh, Dad also said that he has some big news to share tonight?" Anna continued. "Should we be worried?"

An alarm bell sounded in Julia's ears. *Why on earth had Jackson told Anna he had "big news"? Had Jackson told Julia something, something that she'd forgotten? Had her stress over the publishing house and her father's release from prison actually deleted parts of her memory?*

"No, honey. You shouldn't be worried," Julia told Anna coaxingly. "You know how dramatic your father likes to be."

Anna and Rachel laughed good-naturedly, their voices joining together like two parts of a song. Julia's stomach tied itself into sailors' knots. *What on earth would happen next?*

When they pulled into the driveway, Julia pressed the garage door opener to reveal Henry Crawford in the garage, a backpack over his shoulders, a pair of aviator sunglasses covering his eyes, and his hand lifted in a funny wave.

"He's such a clown," Anna commented before she stepped out of the SUV and ran smack-dab into her younger brother for a sloppy hug. Moments later, Rachel joined their group hug, whooping wildly.

Julia watched from the front seat of the SUV, feeling just about a million years old. Her children loved her and adored her, but their true friendships existed between them. Julia hadn't had that with her siblings since the autumn of 1996. Her heart ached for them so much.

*What was Bernard Copperfield doing right that moment?*

*Was he walking along Jetties Beach, gazing out across an ocean he hadn't seen in twenty-five years?*

*Was he eating one of his favorite Nantucket dishes? Clam chowder? Lobster? The croissants from the bakery down the road?*

"Mom! Are you coming?" Henry called as the siblings headed for the back door.

Julia shook out her chaotic thoughts, smiled, and stepped out of the SUV to hug her son. "I missed you..." she cooed.

"Mom, we had lunch like two weeks ago," Henry told her playfully.

"Really, kiddo? One lunch every two weeks, and that's enough for you?" Julia remarked sarcastically, rolling her eyes.

Already, Anna dug through the refrigerator and tugged out one of the more expensive bottles of chardonnay. Henry snapped his fingers and said, "Hook me up with a glass of that, Anna Banana."

"And me!" Rachel called.

"Rachel, come on. You're nineteen..." Julia tried.

At this, her three children giggled and cast one another knowing glances.

"Mom, you know what happens at college, right?" Anna asked.

"There's no way you didn't drink before you were twenty-one," Henry pointed out, taking a filled glass from Anna. "You had Anna when you were almost twenty-one. And you met Dad when you were..."

"I was nineteen," Julia admitted with a sigh. "And I guess it's possible that your father and I shared a few beers during those early days."

"Yeah, yeah," Rachel shot in a sing-song voice. She then

41

lifted up on her toes to plant a kiss on Julia's cheek, adding, "I always drink responsibly, Mama. Don't you worry about that."

Suddenly, the garage door erupted open, making the entire house vibrate.

"It's Dad!" Anna called, rushing for the door that led to the garage and pulling it open to wave at her father's Camaro.

Julia turned in the opposite direction, grabbed the bottle of chardonnay, and filled a glass. Her stomach clenched into knots. She was letting her nerves get the best of her. *When was the last time she'd looked Jackson Crawford in the eye?* He'd gotten home after midnight the previous night and left that morning at five-fifteen, grunting that he had to head back to Hyde Park. She hadn't yet told him they'd abandoned the Willis Tower offices and that she'd had to fire most of her staff. She hadn't yet told him that her father was out of prison. She felt like an island, unto herself. One that you couldn't find on any map, no matter how hard you searched.

"There they are!" The handsome journalist, Jackson Crawford, stepped into their house with the air of a celebrity entering a crowd of fans. He hugged Anna, then Rachel, before shaking his son's hand and saying, "Thanks again for your help the other day, Henry. The guys at the station liked having you around."

Julia hadn't known that Jackson and Henry had worked together recently. *Why hadn't one of them mentioned this? Why had she been kept in the dark?*

"Hi, there." Jackson sounded like he was speaking to a stranger rather than to his wife, the mother of his three children. He stamped a kiss on her cheek and delivered his magical, dimpled grin. "I see you collected our previous wards from across the country."

"They're all back to take advantage of our hospitality again," Julia said easily, grateful that she'd found some way to joke with him again.

If anything, Jackson knew how to perform. He could have been an actor, yet he thought too much of himself to have a career based on fictional stories.

"What's for dinner?" Jackson asked.

"Clam chowder. Fresh rolls. Corn on the cob," Julia recited.

"Wow. Clam chowder? You haven't made that in years." Jackson's eyes glittered, intrigued. "Someone wants to walk down memory lane."

"I always forget you're from the east coast," Anna said with a flip of her hair. "I just think of us as Midwesterners, through and through."

"Nah, your mother grew up with the elite east coasters," Jackson corrected, pouring himself a glass of wine. "She's not like the rest of us out here."

"I don't know what you mean," Julia countered, her nostrils flaring.

"Ah! I see I touched a nerve." Jackson cleared his throat, then lifted his wine glass. "That's not to say she hasn't worked hard— if not harder than almost anyone I've known in my life. The success at Orchard Publishing is proof of that."

Julia's knees clacked together. She sipped her wine as her children scrambled around her husband, asking him questions about his recent journalistic endeavors, demanding his most wild and inventive tales. Julia turned back toward the clam chowder to add more seasoning. She then removed the corn from the fridge, buttered and salted it, and splayed it across a baking sheet to be roasted in the oven for twenty-five minutes. Her children and husband exchanged fun banter, sounding like a collection of teenagers on the brink of the rest of their lives.

Well— her children were, basically.

*But her husband? Where had this energy come from?*

Forty-five minutes later, the Crawford family sat around the antique dining room table, each with a large bowl of clam chowder, freshly-baked rolls with melted butter, peaches and cream corn on the cob that had melted button and salt atop. The conversation hadn't lagged for a moment, although Julia had mostly performed the part of the bystander, the audience.

"This clam chowder is amazing, Mom," Rachel complimented, closing her eyes as she layered another spoonful into her mouth. "Where did you learn to cook it?"

"My mother, actually..." Julia replied simply, lifting her eyes toward Jackson's. Her heart thudded strangely, threatening to leap from her chest.

She'd never told her children about her parents, or about The Copperfield House, or about her siblings, or even really about Nantucket Island. She suddenly felt she'd misrepresented her entire life, her entire personality. She suddenly felt as though they couldn't possibly know her at all.

"Well, it's awesome," Rachel said. "You have to teach me."

"I will, Rachel..." Julia told her, her voice weak.

There was a strange moment of silence, the first since their arrival back home. Their spoons clinked through their bowls. Henry's teeth tore through his corn on the cob. Julia searched her mind for something, anything to say. But before she could, Anna turned her attention back to her father and asked, "Dad, are you ever going to tell us what secret you have up your sleeves? It's driving me crazy."

"Ah yes." Jackson slid a napkin across his lips. His eyes seemed to purposefully avoid Julia's. "That's quite a surprise."

"Come on... I can't take it," Anna told him.

"All right. Well." Jackson cleared his throat ominously.

And over the next full minute, Julia forgot how to breathe.

"As you all know, my work has been escalating lately," he began. "It's been a unique pleasure working my way up in the Chicago news scene. But I was recently contacted by a news agency in Beijing."

Henry, Anna, and Rachel's jaws dropped open. Julia

remained cool and collected, her spoon poised at the very top of the steaming bowl of clam chowder.

"Beijing?" Anna demanded. "As in... China?"

"It's the only Beijing I know of," Jackson quipped, his grin crooked as he explained more about what he knew. "I'll be covering English news in Beijing for English-speaking locals, focusing on Beijing's international relationship with the rest of the world. It's a stellar opportunity. Certainly, one I couldn't turn down."

Anna, Henry, and Rachel howled with excitement for their father, hugging him and opening another bottle of wine. All the while, Jackson seemed distant toward Julia. Again, she asked herself if she'd ever truly known this man at all.

"I'm so proud of my parents," Anna beamed for the first time at both of them. "You're not like other people. You're both pushing forward in your careers. Making space for each other's projects. I think it's beautiful."

"Isn't it beautiful?" Julia asked tenderly, forcing Jackson to look at her for the first time since his big reveal. She lifted her glass of wine toward him, arching an eyebrow knowingly. "To the future."

* * *

Several hours later, when Henry, Anna, and Rachel headed off to an old friend's house for a get-together, Julia stood like a ghost in the kitchen, a glass of wine pressed against her heart. Jackson remained in the living room with his arms crossed stiffly over his chest. She wanted to tell him something that would hurt him. She wanted to tell him what a stranger he was to her. But words weren't enough in the face of his arrogance.

"If it wasn't clear," Jackson began, "I'd like to go to Beijing by myself."

Julia let out a low haunting laugh. "I got the subtext, Jackson."

"I imagined you did. You're no idiot."

"Glad to hear your opinion of me hasn't completely deteriorated," Julia spat back.

Again, silence. Julia stewed in resentment, both toward him and toward herself. This was the life she'd built for herself in the wake of all that devastation out in Nantucket. Now, with her children gone and her husband hightailing it off to Beijing, she had nothing, all over again.

"When do you leave?" Julia asked him.

"Next week," Jackson replied, his words cold as ice.

*Next week.* Julia blinked at him. He'd known about this change for quite a while and had chosen to keep it from her. He'd kept tight-lipped as he worked on his plans.

There was nothing else to be said. But because Jackson was a chatty Kathy, he continued, adding insult to injury.

"I've thought about being alone again for a long time."

"That's nice to hear, Jackson."

"It's really not you. You're a fantastic woman, Julia."

"Are you going to do the *'it's not you, it's me'* to your wife of twenty years?" Julia demanded. "I thought you were better than that."

"I just want to be clear that I never cheated on you. I never went outside of this. I love our children. And I loved our life."

Julia blinked at him. Why wasn't she running at him with her fists lifted, wailing, and demanding that he stay with her or take her with him? Why wasn't she crying out that she loved him and wanted to fight for this? Did she have any passionate bone left in her body?

"Let's hold off on telling the kids for a little while longer," Jackson recited as though he'd rehearsed this. "I don't want my first few weeks in Beijing to be overloaded with having to call Anna, Henry, and Rachel and explain myself."

"No. " Julia countered. "We wouldn't want your children to affect your career."

"Julia. Don't be like this. Please."

"Like what?" Julia rather enjoyed her newfound cold demeanor. As he gaped at her, she headed for the fridge, grabbed a full bottle of rosé, slipped her glass under her elbow, then turned toward the staircase. "Tell the kids I have a migraine," she shot back at him. "But don't worry. Tomorrow I'll wake up bright and early and cook us all pancakes, eggs, and bacon. We can still pretend to be a unified family for a little longer. Won't that be nice?"

# Chapter Six

The three-bedroom colonial house on Lincoln Avenue was only four or so blocks from The Copperfield House. Twenty-two years ago, when the house had been listed for sale, Charlie Bellows' girlfriend at the time had parked them in front of the white-painted house with its green shutters and big willow tree, taken his hand, and whispered, *"All I've ever wanted was a house like this, one to fill up with children and a whole lot of love."* How could Charlie resist? He'd been broken-hearted for two years by that point. He'd wanted to rebuild his life. And by that time, The Copperfield House was more of a haunted house than anything else. He told himself not to walk down that road if he could help it. He told himself to live and live well.

Twenty-two years after Charlie purchased the place, almost to the day, he awoke in the bed he'd made himself from the oak tree he'd chopped down in his parents' yard before their deaths. He was all alone beneath the scratchy quilt his mother had passed down to him, the one she'd sewn herself during the blizzard of seventy-seven. Unfortunately, it was Sunday, which meant that the day stretched out before him without necessary demands. He appreciated the workdays; he appreciated having something to do with his time.

"Good morning, you old scoundrel." Charlie greeted himself in the bathroom mirror, where he stood shirtless and ragged, rubbing the sleep out of his eyes. He was forty-three years old these days, and he felt he'd lived a mountain of a life. It made his knees ache to think there was still a lot more to go if he was lucky.

Outside, April sunlight glittered through a smattering of clouds. He shrugged himself into a t-shirt and a pair of running pants, then tied his shoelaces slowly before walking out the front door. It was April and still not tourist season; he left the front door unlocked. If there was anything he felt he could trust, it was others on the island of Nantucket.

He knew how ironic that was, especially given what had happened with Bernard Copperfield twenty-five years ago. But in all his years in his place on Lincoln Avenue, where he'd raised two children, he'd never had a single lick of trouble, save for some rowdy tourists who'd kept his girls up too late at night.

Charlie stretched himself out on the sidewalk, trying his darnedest to reach his toes but giving up altogether when he inched just past his knees. It was pathetic. He then walked toward his favorite route along the beach, where he finally lifted his knees through the air, forcing himself through a three-mile run that looped him out and back.

When he finished, he hovered just west of Steps Beach with his hands on his knees. His sweat soaked through his t-shirt, cooling his skin. The waves rushed headlong toward him, cresting into a jagged white peak and falling into nothing against the sand. That very beach would be heavy with sunbathing tourists in just a few months, none of whom could possibly comprehend what it meant to live out the winter months on Nantucket.

Well. It was one thing to live out the winter months. It was another altogether to live out the winter months as a widower.

Unsure why, Charlie continued east down the beach, coming closer to The Copperfield House than he'd been in many years. He'd heard rumors about the old place, of course. The people of Nantucket Island didn't just adore gossip; it was like they ran off it like a car needed gasoline.

The gossip mill had produced the following rumors, none of which could be verified.

**Rumor one:** Greta Copperfield hadn't left The Copperfield House since Bernard had been taken away to prison.

**Rumor two:** None of the Copperfield children had ever returned, not even for Ella's graduation from high school, which everyone said was a "crying shame."

**Rumor three:** Greta Copperfield had taken a much younger lover, who now resided in The Copperfield House with her.

**Rumor four:** The Copperfield House was condemned, but nobody was willing to kick Greta Copperfield out on the street, as nobody knew what her money situation was and whether she could handle it. Plus, hadn't she been through enough?

**Rumor five:** Greta Copperfield had died more than ten years ago, but one of the Copperfield children kept the house in the family— probably Quentin, as he seemed like the one with the most money (given his newfound work as the morning news anchor in New York City).

Charlie stalled on the beach, rolling the tip of his toe through the sand. If he continued to walk just a few more feet, he was bound to see the exterior of The Copperfield House. That gorgeous Victorian home that held so many of his most blissful memories. Those particular memories were untainted by the horrors of time or growing up. They existed without responsibility or aging or bills or the needs of children. They pulsed with the love he'd had for Julia Copperfield— the woman he was supposed to marry all those years ago, the woman he'd lost forever.

"Turn back," he muttered to himself, turning around.

But when he lifted his eyes, he discovered one of the Copperfield neighbors, Ms. Jenkins, making her way toward him. She held a walking stick in one hand, stabbing the sand beneath her to hold her gait. Charlie had seen her around town over the years, inching closer and closer toward old age, usually wrapped in several hand-knitted sweaters. Back when he'd been a consistent visitor at The Copperfield House, she'd been in her early fifties, which probably made her nearly eighty years old.

"Charlie Bellows! Is that you?"

Charlie hadn't spoken to anyone in many days. Most of his weeks were spent with limited communication, usually only with the secretary at the woodworking studio, where he designed hand-carved wooden furnishings for the rich tourists of Nantucket Island. *Come on, Charlie. It's a simple answer. It's yes.*

"You heard what's happened?" Ms. Jenkins seemed unwilling to wait around for him to come up with something to say.

"Um. I guess not." Finally, his words came out.

Ms. Jenkins looked overwhelmingly pleased to deliver this news. She lifted a finger to bring him closer while her eyes remained somewhere back behind him, perhaps even toward The Copperfield House.

"Bernard Copperfield is back," she whispered, her voice witch-like.

A shiver raced up and down Charlie's spine. When the judge had given him twenty-five years in prison, Charlie had envisioned twenty-five years to be nearly one hundred.

"Have you seen him?" he asked her.

She shook her head. "No, but a friend passed by and said she saw him smoking that pipe of his out the window."

"I see." Charlie's throat tightened fearfully. "And what about Greta? Have you seen her?"

Ms. Jenkins pressed her finger against her lips knowingly. "She's an even greater mystery, isn't she? Always latched away in that house. Waiting for something to happen. Or maybe... waiting for him to come back, so she can get her revenge."

Charlie wanted to roll his eyes into the back of his head. Still, he could sense that the older lady believed this garbage. It was all gossip. He couldn't argue with her.

"Think about it," Ms. Jenkins continued. "Bernard was the only man she ever loved. He got her pregnant when they lived in Paris, so she had to give up her dream of living in France. Then, he stole millions from their dearest friends, slept with the young writer living in their house, and left her to fend for herself for the last twenty-five years."

"It's quite a story," Charlie replied, his shoulders falling forward.

Ms. Jenkins stitched her eyebrows together thoughtfully, analyzing him. "Weren't you involved with one of the Copperfield girls years ago when you were in high school?"

"Not sure what you mean?" Charlie told her.

Ms. Jenkins' eyes stormed with curiosity. Finally, she shook her head so that her grey hair quaked around her ears. "No, I must be making it all up. You were married to Sally. God rest her soul." Ms. Jenkins then stepped closer, placed her hand on the top of Charlie's shoulder, and said, "Those girls of yours are lucky to have a father like you. The poor Copperfields. The poor, poor Copperfield children."

With that, Ms. Jenkins stabbed her walking stick back in the sand and pushed her way back down the beach, away from Charlie. Charlie was left with stones in his belly.

On his walk back to the house on Lincoln Avenue, his

mind raced with countless images. It was like Ms. Jenkins had turned on the television of his innermost memories. They flashed through his mind like they'd happened only yesterday.

Charlie and Julia, hand-in-hand at the beach.

Charlie and Julia sharing a strawberry milkshake as the summer light faded around them.

Charlie and Julia sharing every single conceivable "first" with one another, from holding hands to kissing and beyond.

Charlie and Julia, packing their bags on that fateful April night, headed off the island and toward the rest of their lives.

It was supposed to be Charlie and Julia, always and forever.

Back in the house on Lincoln, Charlie showered and dressed in a pair of jeans and a soft gray t-shirt. He sat in his armchair, a book in his lap, blinking into space. He knew that reading would take his mind off the inevitable darkness that stirred within, but his arms remained limp.

He missed her.

*His wife? Yes, his wife.* He missed her so desperately sometimes that he felt his heart might shatter. Sally had been a real love, a steadfast love. It had never been a surprising or an electric love or a love that had made him weak in the knees— but a love that involved breakfasts, dinners, tender kisses, and soft, lazy nights in bed. When Sally had passed away so suddenly from cancer, Charlie had gazed at the empty spot of the bed, his arms heavy to his sides. *"What am I going to do now?"* he remembered asking the space around him as though it would answer back.

A photograph on the far wall reflected the beautiful images of Sally with their twin daughters, Zoey and Willa. He'd taken the photograph three years ago, just a few months before the cancer diagnosis. In the photo, it seemed they all knew their time together was coming to an abrupt end. They seemed to hold onto one another tighter, to grin extra wider. *"One more, for the good times."*

God, he missed them all.

But Julia, well... He'd gone his entire life missing her and would probably continue missing her forever.

It wasn't like Charlie hadn't searched for Julia on social media and learned all he could. It was the modern age, wasn't it? Plus, Charlie had plenty of time on his hands to "surf the web," as he didn't like to hang around with other Nantucket residents. Gossip wasn't his thing, and without his wife and daughters around, he felt like a weight to others around. What could he possibly offer? It wasn't like he could bake a pie.

This was what he'd learned.

After Julia and Charlie had broken up, she'd somehow made her way to Chicago, where she'd had her first daughter about a year before Zoey and Willa had been born. After that, she'd had two more children with the same guy, who she married around the same time. *Jackson something?* It was a mouthful of a name, whatever it was. Somehow during those early days of motherhood, she'd managed to finish her high school and college degrees and start her own publishing house, which had slowly inched through the ranks of the publishing world. Based on his most recent searches (during a very weak moment around a year ago), Charlie had learned that her publishing house had offices in the Willis Tower, the tallest building in Chicago.

Julia Copperfield had asked him to run away with her, leave the island of Nantucket for good and build a life with her.

What had happened next had shattered his world.

He leaned his head back, forcing himself to take deep breaths. When anxiety had taken hold of him, Sally had held his hands tenderly and asked him to tell her what he knew.

This, she'd told him, would ground him to reality. This would remind him he was okay.

"These are the things I know, Sally..." he began tentatively, feeling like a foolish man in conversation with a woman who'd died two years ago. "I know that we built a beautiful life together, one I am grateful for every day. I know that our daughters, Zoey and Willa, are considerate, honest, and intelligent women with their lives ahead of them. I know that I am a rather good carpenter with high-paying clients who seek me out to build furniture for them. But..."

Charlie's voice crackled. He sounded like an idiot, didn't he? What kind of man sat around complimenting his skills on a lonely Sunday afternoon? He reached for the remote and flicked on the television, hunting for an action, sci-fi, or thriller movie, anything to take his mind off his reality. If Sally had been there, she'd have said, *"Why don't we just enjoy the silence together? I love the wind off the ocean. I love these afternoons with just you."*

# Chapter Seven

R achel was the last Crawford child to head back to where she'd come from. As Jackson had to return to Chicago to close out the last of his American-based stories, Julia found herself alone at the bus station in the rain, watching as her youngest daughter trudged back on the steaming bus and collapsed in one of the last rows. Rachel lifted a hand to say goodbye through the bus window, and Julia found herself almost manic as she waved her hand back and forth. She was reminded of when Rachel went to kindergarten for the first time— her last baby headed out into the world alone. How it had shattered her! Jackson hadn't understood it and insisted that Julia had a problem "letting go." Julia had laughed at that. She'd left her entire life in Nantucket behind, hadn't she? Didn't that count for something?

Back at the house that she and Jackson had shared for more than twenty years, Julia moved into the guest bedroom, where she piled a collection of books and notepads on the antique desk and prepared herself for what she called "Julia time." With her husband preparing for Beijing, her children out across the country, and her publishing house dwindling to nothing, it was time for Julia to ask herself what was next.

It was finally time to write that book.

Finally, time to put her work where her heart was.

But when she positioned her fingers on the computer keys in preparation to write out the first line, there came a colossal roar from downstairs.

Julia leaped up and rushed to the landing above the staircase, where she peered down to discover none other than her handsome husband, who'd returned home from chasing his story to blare his favorite albums from high school on the speaker system. Previously, Julia had only used the speaker system to play Chopin, Beethoven, and Vivaldi. With Nirvana blaring out, their modern cookie-cutter family home seemed like a college house for fraternity brothers.

"Can you turn it down?" Julia hollered to her husband.

Jackson lifted his chin and tapped his ear. "What?"

Infuriated, Julia arched an eyebrow, tilted her head, then screamed, "TURN. IT. DOWN."

"Jesus..." Jackson breathed as he spun the volume knob slightly to the left.

"Don't worry, honey. I'm sure they'll let you play 'Smells Like Teen Spirit' as loud as you want over in Beijing," she told him

The words Jackson muttered after that weren't ones Julia wanted to hear.

Jackson raised the volume back up when she returned to the guest bedroom. The base was so loud the house quivered around her. Julia sat once more at the computer, her fingers on the keys as she blinked at the blank page.

*How had she written back in high school?*

*Here we are now. Entertain us...*

The words of Kurt Cobain's iconic song rattled through her skull. She placed her hands over her ears and rolled her shoulders forward. Had she ever had a creative bone in her body? Maybe she was incapable of creativity.

Julia slept fitfully that night, telling herself that she would begin her creative writing pursuits in the morning. It was the first Monday in memory that she wasn't forced to travel to Chicago city-center for her job at the publishing house. This gave her more than two hours of extra time per day. Two hours! That was ten extra hours per week. She lay beneath the crisp sheets of the guest bed and listened to the familiar pattern of Jackson as he prepared to leave for work. There was the rush of the shower, the buzz of his electric razor, and the higher-pitched buzz of his electric toothbrush. Due to his recent television appearances, Jackson's vanity had mounted, requiring nearly forty-five minutes of preparation time before he finally headed out the door to grab his stupid Camaro and drive it out of sight.

Julia jumped out of bed and walked into the kitchen, feeling like a ghost within her own home. As the liquid bubbled into the coffee pot, she scrolled through her phone and forced herself not to text any of her children. Maybe she could reach out to a friend in the area? She had a couple from when the kids had been in high school, plus a handful in the publishing industry. But of course, those in the publishing industry most certainly knew about her publishing house's demise. Pitying eyes were the worst sort of eyes. She remembered them from the trial on Nantucket Island back in 1997, and she certainly didn't want to relive them now.

Julia made herself a bowl of yogurt with berries and bananas, then poured herself a mug of coffee. Midway through the pour, it again hit her that her marriage was as good as over. It was a strange sensation. *Should she email a divorce lawyer? No. Maybe Jackson would get to China and realize he'd made a mistake.*

*But did she plan to go back to some guy who'd taken a job in China without telling her about it?*

No.

Nobody had ever eaten yogurt with berries and bananas as angrily as she did. She scooped them violently, crunching the berries with the sharp tips of her teeth. When she went back upstairs, the white brilliance of her boring guest room nearly destroyed her. She had to get out of there.

She couldn't stand to be in that house a moment longer.

A few years ago, Julia and Jackson had decided to purchase expensive luggage, saying that it would "last them forever." Now, Julia tugged both enormous suitcases out from the hall closet and began to fill them with her things— jeans, sweatshirts, dresses, stockings, skirts, turtlenecks, and plenty of shoes. She took more than twenty books, unwilling to let them linger in that poisonous house alone. She then grabbed several bottles of expensive wine from the wine cellar, which she and Jackson had "collected for later celebrations," stuffed the suitcases in the back of the SUV, showered, and then spent forty minutes perfecting her style.

The woman who sat in the driver's seat of the SUV snapped a selfie of herself and contemplated the image.

Was that Julia Copperfield, the young woman who'd run away from Nantucket in April 1997?

It was, but a different version altogether.

Julia eased out of the driveway and paused to watch the garage door close for a final time. She imagined herself like Carrie in that Stephen King book, burning the house down behind her. Somehow, some way, Jackson would find a way to profit off the insurance money if she did that. *Better not,* she thought to herself

After her surprise pregnancy, Julia had become a very cautious driver. Her kids teased her endlessly, suggesting that little old ladies could out-race her if they tried. Rage stirred in the base of Julia's belly, one that forced her foot on the pedal and thrust her out of Bartlett and out of Illinois, maybe even forever.

Tears flowed freely as she breezed east, whipping along the state line between Michigan and Indiana before gliding into Ohio. The tears seemed to loosen her up, to open her eyes to the beauty of her surroundings and truly make sense of what she'd done.

With every passing moment, she felt more and more sure of her decision to get out of Chicago.

Around five-thirty that evening, Julia arrived in Buffalo, New York and breezed off the highway and directly into a parking spot next to a mid-grade hotel. Had Jackson been beside her, he'd have said something searing about the hotel, that it was bug-infested or only sold bad, sweet wine. But to Julia, who was finally alone in the world, high off her belief in her power and ability to run away, this mid-grade hotel was akin to heaven itself.

Julia checked herself into Room 377, where she washed her hands and face and reapplied her makeup. Once finished, she headed back downstairs to sit in the hotel restaurant with a glass of rosé, which wasn't as bad as her imaginary version of what Jackson had anticipated and watched.

The travelers who stopped at this hotel were a mixed bag. There was a family of four in the corner, squabbling over which pizzas to order from the restaurant. An older couple sat to their left, holding hands across the table as their food cooled. It seemed they never ran out of anything to say to one another. It struck Julia that perhaps, even into their seventies, they met at that hotel and had a romantic affair. Maybe they had partners elsewhere. Maybe they'd been doing it for years.

*Were all "official" relationships doomed? Or was she just cynical based on her experiences?*

"Can I grab you something to eat?" A waiter arrived, flicking his gum from one side of his mouth to the other.

Julia ordered a panini with mozzarella and tomato sauce and a bag of chips. Before he made his way back to the kitchen, she asked for another glass of wine, which he promptly returned. This was her night alone in a strange place; she wanted to make the edges of her vision just the slightest bit foggy. She didn't want to think that Jackson hadn't called at all. She knew he wouldn't notice her absence for another few days when he needed someone to drop him off at the airport to head to Beijing. That was the thing with Jackson. He gave you his attention when he needed something.

As Julia settled deeper into her restaurant booth, another family of six walked in— two parents, three girls, and an older boy who seemed to use his age and experience over his other siblings.

Julia froze, her glass of wine lifted in mid-air.

It could have been them.

It could have been the Copperfields from another time.

The two younger girls lingered behind the others, pausing at the vending machine in the corner and digging through their little coin purses. Their mother called back, "Don't ruin your dinner!" But already, the youngest stuck a quarter into the latch, giggling madly. When they retrieved a bright orange Reese's package from the belly of the machine, they tore it open, placing one of each chocolate coin across the palms of their hands.

Julia blinked back tears that threatened to fall.

But the scene seemed too familiar. The girls could have been Julia and Ella back in 1995, just before Ella's moody blues pushed her deeper into her musical universe and just before Julia took off to build another life.

"Girls! I would save those if I were you," their mother told them.

"Ah, let them eat dessert first," their father offered with a laugh. "Life's too short not to eat dessert first, isn't it?"

"Don't you get any ideas, Reggie. You know what the doctor said about your cholesterol." Life can be a whole lot shorter if you—" The woman spoke sharply to her husband, her face lined with fear.

"I know what the doctor said. I'll order the salad tonight, just like I told you I would." The husband sighed, slightly exasperated, even as he placed a kiss on his wife's cheek. "Girls. You heard your mother. Healthy food first. Then, dessert."

*Was this what a marriage was supposed to be?* Julia wondered. Forcing one another to make healthy choices, if only because you wanted each other to stick around the world a little longer?

"I know what the doctor said. I'll order the salad tonight, just like I told you I would."

Julia hardly touched her panini. The waiter returned after thirty minutes and asked if she wanted it to be remade for her if it hadn't been up to her standards. Julia nearly leaped from her skin with surprise.

"Oh, no. I'll eat the rest," she lied to him.

The family charged the food bill on their room and headed back upstairs, the eldest boy hovering behind, his hands stuffed in his pockets. The over-sugared youngest girls scampered up ahead, twirling in front of the elevators with their arms outstretched.

*Where would this family be in twenty-five years? Would the two little girls remember these moments of chocolate and elevator twirls? Would they gather for Christmas and call one another on their birthdays? Would anything matter at all?*

Back upstairs, Julia splayed back on the hotel bed and tried not to think of how many other lonesome souls had slept in that bed, wondering where their lives were headed.

With her phone lifted over her head, she hunted down the

website for the indie rock band Pottersville. The head photograph on the page featured a thirty-something version of Ella alongside her on-again, off-again boyfriend, the rockstar, Will Ashton. Two other musicians, who seemed to rotate in and out of the band over the years, also scowled in the photograph.

Ella. Ella Copperfield.

*What did Ella think of Bernard Copperfield's release from prison after all this time?*

*And what would she think about Julia's trek east?*

**FOR BOOKING AND INQUIRIES: (752) 555-4765**

Shivering, Julia dialed the number and listened as it rang out across the New York night. She couldn't envision what her little sister's life was like over in Brooklyn, New York City. It was endlessly hip, with nearly no relation to Julia's cookie-cutter life in the suburbs of Chicago.

"Hello. This is Will Ashton."

Julia's heart pounded in her throat. She shot upright in bed, stuttering, "Hi. Hello. Um." Here he was, the father of Julia's niece and nephew. A man she'd never met.

"Hello?" Will laughed timidly, good-naturedly.

"Sorry, hi. I'm calling to reach Ella. I wonder if she's around?"

"Ah. She's not here right now, but I can pass along a number for you."

"That would be fantastic, thanks."

Will recited the number to her without question. Julia wrote it down with a shaky hand, thanked him, then called Ella before she could chicken out. She answered on the third ring.

"Hello, this is Ella Copperfield speaking."

Copperfield. The name rang out across the phone lines. Julia nearly froze with disbelief.

"Hello?"

"Ella," Julia breathed. "It's me. It's Julia."

Ella was quiet for a long time. In the background, there was the hum of a television. Julia tried to envision what sort of program Ella watched at the end of a long day. The nineties-era MTV she'd been glued to was no more.

"Julia..." Ella didn't sound exactly pleased. "How did you get this number?"

"I called the number on your website," Julia replied. Her heart drummed in her chest as she tucked a strand of hair behind her ear, waiting for a reply.

"I see. And Will gave you my personal one."

"He did."

Ella grunted as though she wanted to say more but held herself back. "What can I help you with, Julia?"

Julia wasn't sure what she'd expected from this call. She'd wanted Ella to be the refuge she'd envisioned all sisters to be later in life after you'd gone through the texture of time together.

"Did you hear that Dad was released from prison?"

"I caught something about it, yeah."

"What do you think of it?" Julia asked.

"What am I supposed to think about it, Julia?" Ella sounded exasperated, just about as sick of the world as Julia felt.

"I would think you'd have some feelings about it," Julia told her.

"Well, I don't."

Julia's nostrils flared. After a deep breath, she said, "I'm driving to Nantucket right now."

Ella's voice was sharp. "Are you insane?" It was a rhetorical question.

Julia blinked back tears. "I saw Dad on the news. He looked so old, Ella. He's seventy-one now, and I'm starting to feel like..."

"Like what? Like you shouldn't have abandoned all of us like that?"

They shared the silence after that. Julia knew Ella had a right to these words, but that didn't mean they didn't sting.

"I'll get there by tomorrow night," Julia added.

Ella sighed. "I should warn you. Mom's different these days."

"Mom? You've seen her?"

"Well, yeah. Not often, but yeah. Sometimes when Will and I go on tour, she watches the kids for us, either here in Brooklyn or there in Nantucket. When she's here I always beg her to stay. I tell her that that stupid house is haunted, poisoning her, but she always returns. And then, like clock-work, all that loneliness drives her crazy again."

Julia closed her eyes against another wave of emotion, of sorrow. Greta Copperfield knew Ella's children; she was a grandmother to them. But for Anna, Henry, and Rachel, Julia had made sure they hardly knew Greta's name.

"Isn't that even more of a reason that we should go to The Copperfield House and help out?" Julia asked timidly. "Mom's depression and Dad's return from prison?"

"Julia..." Ella sounded at a loss. "I don't know what's gotten into you. I don't know what your life's like and why you left it again. But the truth is, it's been twenty-five years. Whatever your mission is with this, it doesn't sound like it's actually about Mom and Dad. It sounds like it's all about you. Don't involve me. I have enough going on in New York."

With that, Ella Copperfield hung up.

# Chapter Eight

April 1997

"Let's read off the checklist a final time." Shaggy-haired Charlie opened his notepad, furrowing his brow.

"We don't have time, Charlie. The ferry leaves in fifteen minutes. We'll barely make it."

Charlie's cheeks burned red with embarrassment and fear. Julia could sense his emotions. She knew him inside and out.

"Fine, Charlie. Let's read the checklist one more time..." Julia dropped back on her childhood bed and listened as The Copperfield House creaked around them, breaking against the rush of the April wind.

"Okay. First off. Money?"

"Everything we have to our names. Check."

Julia had cleared out her bank account just that afternoon, explaining to the bank teller that she, her mother, and her little sister, Ella, planned to leave the island shortly to get away from the "public eye." The teller had been grateful for this tidbit of gossip and whispered, "Of course, honey. It's been such a trying time for your family." She'd then splayed four-hundred and seventeen dollars across Julia's palms.

Charlie had kept all his lawn mowing money in a piggy bank on his dresser. He'd taken five-hundred and sixty-seven dollars from it, an impressive feat for a teenager.

"Passports," Charlie spouted.

"Check."

"Driver's licenses," Charlie added.

"Check. Come on, Charlie. Let's get on with it..."

"Clothing. Toiletries..."

"We can buy anything we forgot, Charlie."

"Journals. Books."

"Check and check." Julia leaped from her bed and laced her fingers through Charlie's. His pulse was quick, like an anxious rabbit's. "We're going to be just fine, Charlie. We have each other, don't we? What else could we possibly need?"

Charlie closed his eyes as Julia kissed him tenderly on the lips. Somewhere deep in The Copperfield House came the sound of Greta Copperfield weeping. The television in the downstairs living room blared a soap opera, and outside, a bird squawked, projecting doom and gloom across the place. Julia thought if she remained in that house a moment longer, she might suffocate.

It was her prison, just as much as the one in upstate New York had become her father's.

Julia and Charlie kicked up their heels as they raced for the ferry outside. Their backpacks smacked their backs ominously, thudding away against their spring jackets. On high, clouds rolled out into dark blues and blacks, groaning over the Atlantic.

Julia tried to take stock of the island as they ran. Down Beach Street, past Easton, along the playground, past the Nantucket Yacht Club. Outside the Yacht Club, the men her father had stolen from sat outside in the last rays of sunlight, puffing on pipes. The white fabric of their t-shirt was nearly blinding; their shoes had been worn no more than one or two times. Julia wanted to race up to them, to demand if they were happy after what they'd done. *"You destroyed my family!"*

But no, a voice in the back of her head reminded her. They simply told the truth to a jury of their peers.

In truth, the only person who'd destroyed the Copperfield family was Bernard Copperfield himself.

And they were left with the trash-heap of what he'd done.

"There!" Julia whipped a finger out to point to the ferry, which still purred against the side of the dock. They paused at the ticket operator table, where they purchased two five-dollar tickets to Hyannis Port.

The minute they stepped onto the ferry, the ferry operator unlatched the ramp from the dock and clicked it back into place on the side of the boat. Julia gasped with surprise at the finality of the sound. They were no longer attached to the island she'd always called her home. They now floated with reckless abandon, off to the next phase of their lives.

Overwhelmed yet swimming with unbridled love, Julia rushed into Charlie's arms and kissed him passionately— no longer like a teenager with nothing to lose but like a woman, afraid of what would happen next. She felt Charlie's fear, too. It swam through him and poured over her, joining with hers.

"It's going to be all right," Julia whispered, unsure if she spoke to Charlie or more to herself.

\* \* \*

When the ferry arrived at Hyannis Port, Charlie and Julia stepped out and, with mild shrugs, began to walk toward the bus station. Their general plan had been "New York City," as it seemed utterly romantic and where you were "meant" to go if you were a runaway.

At the bus station, a woman with a visor wrapped tightly across her forehead told them the next bus to New York left at three in the afternoon. This gave them four hours to walk around with their backpacks, eat the snacks they'd packed from the cabinets of The Copperfield House, and a chance to write poems, which they read to one another in the bus terminal.

Julia read a simplistic poem with stuttered syllables and wide eyes.

I think we're
About to start the
Rest of our lives
together.
Just like
We always
Dreamed
We would.

Perhaps because it still felt like an adventure, that first week in New York City was the dream Julia had hoped it would be. They rented a bunk bed in a ten-bed dorm in a hostel in Greenwich Village for four dollars per night and wandered the glorious streets as spring flourished around them. They lived off coffee and cigarettes, toast and poetry, and snuck into several museums, spending long hours before iconic paintings and photographs that had changed art history forever.

On April 17th, Julia celebrated her eighteenth birthday in Central Park, where she and Charlie shared a slice of cheese-cake and watched a juggler perfecting his act as a light rain drizzled down upon them.

"Do you miss any of them?" Charlie asked as they continued to watch the juggler.

"Not at all," Julia lied.

Around that time, a hanging pamphlet outside the hostel dorm advertised a studio apartment not far from there, which Julia jumped on without asking Charlie's opinion first.

"Whatever it is, it'll be perfect for us," Julia explained as she dragged him toward the home she'd already put the down payment on.

Charlie's face twitched with doubt. He remained wordless yet followed after her. Where else could he possibly go?

Lucky for them, the studio apartment was reasonable, if tiny. After scouring its corners, closets, and bathroom, Charlie announced, "No cockroaches accounted for." They then collapsed in the center of the single room, with Julia's head on Charlie's chest and their eyes toward the shadows of the ceiling above them.

"This is our home," Julia breathed simply, her heart thudding with a mix of sorrow and excitement.

After all, her home used to be The Copperfield House.

But that was in the past. And this would have to do for now.

They got jobs. It wasn't too difficult to do, as they were both eighteen and had unlimited time to devote to any given restaurant or coffee shop or local movie theater. Julia began to waitress at a high-scale restaurant several blocks down the road. On a good night, she'd make anywhere from one-hundred to two-hundred dollars in tips while Charlie worked two part-time jobs. He was a busboy at another high-scale restaurant and a ticket seller at a movie theater that showed Japanese action movies and sorrowful indie movies from places like Italy and Portugal. On Julia's off days, she liked to go to the movie theater, eat free popcorn, and watch one film after another while Charlie killed time in the seller booth.

Their love was different in New York City. It still felt like it belonged to them, but also like they had to carry it with more tenderness, as though the harsh world around them threatened to break it. They had their first fight in many years during the second week of their stay at the studio apartment when a mouse darted out from a kitchen cabinet and ran directly through Julia's feet. The fight had nothing at all to do with the mouse and rather about the fear Charlie suddenly had about his future as "an adult without a high school education and no prospects in the real world." The mouse had maybe reminded Charlie that without his education, he would struggle through life, live in apartments he couldn't afford, and be unable to put nutritious food on the table.

"If you want to go back and walk across the stage as a graduate of Nantucket High School, be my guest," Julia howled back. "But I'm staying here. I'll date some hot-shot businessman and work my way up in the art world, selling my poems and making enormous paintings that are bigger than this room. And all the while, you'll be on Nantucket, cradling your stupid high school diploma and wishing you'd stayed here with me."

The words were cruel. Julia wished she could go back through time and take them back. She'd had no right to talk to him like that. He'd been nothing but supportive of her. Immediately after, she hugged Charlie as hard as she could and wept, telling him that they could look into getting their GEDs together in a few months' time— that they were smart enough to figure this all out together.

"I couldn't do this without you," she breathed through tears. "I've loved you since I met you. I never want to live without you."

Charlie adored her. He counted every penny of his bus-boy tips, collected all of his paychecks from the movie theater, and put everything toward what they called *"The Julia and Charlie Fund."* Julia did the same with her money. Their rent was seven-hundred and fifty dollars a month, nothing to scoff at— but they managed it that first month and even the second. They ate noodles, pizzas, and crackers with cheap cheeses and frequently bought wine with a fake ID Charlie's cousin had given him the previous summer.

"I think we might be the luckiest people in the entire

world," Julia said once, seated on the mattress they'd placed on the floor of their studio apartment.

"It's nice not to sleep on the floor anymore," Charlie affirmed with a laugh. "I'll give you that."

Julia lifted herself on her knees, closed her eyes, and kissed him gently. "I love you. I love our silly life in the city. And I know it's just going to keep getting better and better."

Julia had no idea that Charlie kept in contact with his parents back in Nantucket. She stupidly and selfishly assumed that her decision to cut all communication mirrored his.

In the middle of June, two months after they arrived in New York City, Julia arrived home late from her shift at the restaurant to discover Charlie wide awake at the kitchen counter, his eyes lined red. A beer was cracked open before him, sweating against the summer heat, which was all the more gruesome in the city's center.

"Charlie... are you okay?"

Charlie shook his head ominously. He sipped his beer and clacked it back on the counter as his shoulders shuddered with sorrow.

Julia stepped toward him slowly, as though he was a bomb about to go off. "What's going on?"

After a long and horrible pause, he whispered, "My mom's sick."

Julia's stomach twisted at his words, as it always did when the world around her shifted off its axis. "What do you mean? How do you know?"

Charlie explained that he'd called home about once a week since they'd arrived, just to check-in. Julia wanted to ridicule him for doing this. She wanted to demand why he'd hidden this fact from her. But instead, she listened as Charlie explained his mother had received another routine check-up a week before, which had escalated to a series of tests and then the discovery of a blood infection called sepsis.

"It's gotten really bad," Charlie explained, his voice cracking. "They aren't sure if she'll make it."

"Oh my God." Julia splayed a hand over her mouth, her stomach heavy with the weight of this truth.

It felt like Nantucket had reached out a hand to grab them and tug them back to where they belonged.

"We have to go back," Charlie explained simply. "I can't just go work at the movie theater and the restaurant, knowing my mom might not make it through this."

Silence swelled through their studio apartment, echoing across their mattress on the floor, the little lamp in the corner, and the box of opened crackers under the cabinet.

"Why don't you just go and see her?" Julia suggested, her voice cracking. "And then come back?"

Charlie groaned inwardly and dropped his chin toward his chest. Julia crossed her arms tightly over her chest. In her purse sat one-hundred and fifteen dollars in crumpled tips. *She'd killed herself for those tips. Was Charlie asking her to just give up everything she'd worked for?*

"Come on, Julia. Look at this place..." Charlie whispered, flailing a hand in the general direction of the mattress. "Don't you remember what we used to have on the island? The ocean and the food, the wind, the sailboats and..."

"Charlie, come on. You're upset. I get it." Julia stepped around the counter and pressed a hand across his chest. "Your mom is a fighter, and she'll pull through this. And when she does, we'll continue to fight for our dreams here in the city."

Charlie's voice cracked as he searched for his answer. His eyes were glossy with sorrow. Finally, he managed, "I just don't know, Julia. I don't know."

Julia forced herself to breathe. She inhaled, then exhaled. She took a slight step back, feeling woozy. She hadn't eaten throughout her shift at the restaurant, unwilling to pause for a moment while her tables waited, eager to tip her unless she proved herself unworthy.

"Okay. Okay. Okay. Let's um. Let's not jump to any sort of conclusion. Your mom is sick. I get that. I understand that. Why don't you just... Go to Nantucket... without me. And then call me when you get there."

"How will I call you?" Charlie asked.

"The restaurant. You can leave a message if I'm not around," she told him. "And I'll call you when I can from wherever I am. Maybe by the time you get back, I'll have a phone set up in this apartment."

"You should come with me, Julia. What your father did has nothing to do with you. Nantucket will continue to adore you, just as they always have."

"I can't, Charlie. It's not even about my father. It's about my pride, now."

Charlie blinked several times as the realization that she wouldn't come back with him sunk in. They shared a long and horrible moment of silence. And then, Charlie stepped forward, swallowing her up in a hug she would remember for the rest of her life.

It was a hug of complete, unadulterated love and understanding.

It was also a hug that meant goodbye.

The following day, when Julia walked Charlie to the bus station, there was an air of finality, as though both knew they wouldn't see one another again. Julia tried to memorize every crease of his face when he smiled, every strand of his dark blonde hair, and the air of his laughter. She tried to remember the ache of her heart, which had beat only with love for him since her thirteenth year. But she knew that soon, so much of that memory would fade out and become just another story of her life.

Just one year after Charlie left New York City, a young and

fast-talking journalism student from Columbia would walk into the restaurant where Julia worked, ordered one martini after another, and finally ask her out on a date. As it turned out, Jackson Crawford was her future— not Charlie Bellows. What a strange journey life would lead her on.

# Chapter Nine

The salty winds off the Atlantic erupted through Julia's dark locks. Julia curled her fingers over the edge of the ferry railing, her feet shoulder-width apart as the vibrations from the ferry motor buzzed through her. It was April, still too early for tourist season, which meant that the ferry was almost empty, its plastic seats downstairs glowing with the gray light of the late spring afternoon. Julia didn't wish to sit, not after that colossal drive across one-half of the continent. Besides, she wanted to lift her chin to the horizon and watch that island move closer to her, growing larger and more real. It was like staring at something that scared you until it no longer did— or until you could convince yourself it meant nothing to you any longer.

Over the years, she and Jackson had been to many seaside resorts and coastal cities— places like Portugal, Sicily, Los Angeles, Seattle, and little coastal towns on the Gulf of Mexico. Since Jackson had taken the job out in Chicago, she'd come to avoid treks to the east coast, save for a few business trips in New York City. Once, Jackson's colleagues had invited them to summer with them on Martha's Vineyard, the island directly next to Nantucket. Jackson had pleaded with her to "let her past go." Julia had scoffed. In the end, Jackson had spent nearly a month on Martha's Vineyard without Julia or their children, sailing across the Vineyard Sound, eating seafood, and probably "living the life of a handsome, career-driven middle-aged man."

He'd said he'd never cheated on her. *But did Julia believe it?*

*Did it matter at all?*

The Nantucket ferry lowered its ramp onto the docks at just past three-thirty in the afternoon. Julia waited in her SUV in the belly of the ferry, watching the cars slowly exit. The local radio station rang into her speakers, playing a song from 2006—nine years after Julia had left Nantucket for good. In 2006, she'd had three young children, the beginning of a career in the publishing industry, and a past she didn't like to stare at too hard for fear it might reach out from the depths of her memories and grab her.

Yet, here she was, chasing it down again.

Julia drove off the ferry, her tires clunking on the metal ramp before easing her toward the main road. Every image before her— the children's park, the lighthouse, and the Yacht Club seemed to have been ripped directly from her dreams. Her heart thrust itself against her ribcage, threatening to fall out to the SUV floor.

Everything seemed lined with sunlight and beauty, with shimmering nostalgia and hopes for a brighter tomorrow.

This was the world Julia had fled twenty-five years ago, the world she'd felt had chewed her up and spat her out.

But it was only now, as she drove slowly through the center of town, that she mourned all she'd lost. When she'd left at the age of seventeen (days before her eighteenth birthday), she'd been unwilling and unable to look back for fear that it would drag her under. When Charlie had returned to Nantucket to be with his mother, Julia hadn't allowed herself to think much of the island. Yes, she'd thought of Charlie— she'd ached for him, wept for him, and even begged him to return to New York City. But when his mother's illness had stretched on for six months and showed no sign of letting up, Julia had finally ended it between her and Charlie. She'd felt the strings of her heart tugging her back to him, to the island, and she couldn't allow it.

*Was Charlie still on the island somewhere?* Julia hadn't allowed herself to look him up online. She'd been a full believer in self-protection, letting what happened in the past, stay in the past. If she let herself look up Charlie Bellows, wouldn't that mean she regretted the life she'd built with Jackson?

*Again, she supposed that didn't matter any longer, either.*

The feel of driving the SUV she'd purchased back in Bartlett there on the street she'd grown up on was surreal. Julia's fingers tightened over the steering wheel as she took her time driving up to the beachfront Victorian home, The Copperfield House, where as, they'd once said in a pamphlet for the artist residency, *"all artistic dreams come true."*

The first sight of the old place nearly shattered Julia's heart.

In the previous twenty-five years, The Copperfield House had fallen into a state of disarray, bordering on all-out dilapidation. She wouldn't have been surprised if someone had labeled it *"condemned."* The remaining shutters hung crooked on either side of the windows, some of which were broken, and the roof required a complete overhaul. The garden twisted angrily, spitting out weeds that looked like they belonged on other planets. The trees, too, seemed sinister, entirely unlike the beautiful ones that had flourished in her youth.

Julia parked her SUV alongside the curb about half a block from the house, wanting to distance herself from the place just in case she chickened out and wanted to escape. She stood before it, feeling dwarfed by the old place— by its time, memories, and ghosts.

Hundreds of writers, artists, musicians, and filmmakers had stood in that spot. They had beamed up at the old structure, filled with promise for the weeks ahead— weeks of endless creativity, good conversation, and delicious food cooked by Greta Copperfield herself.

Julia had been many different versions of herself in that place: a little girl with a scabbed knee from a bicycle fall; a twelve-year-old with a daydreaming problem; a teenager with a journal filled with poetry and a hungry love for her boyfriend, Charlie.

Beyond that, she'd been a daughter, a sister.

She'd been a Copperfield.

There was a clicking sound of a lighter from above. Julia pulled her chin up to catch sight of an older man in the upstairs window, leaning out with a pipe between his lips. His gray-white hair ruffled with the springtime wind. Soon after, smoke from his pipe billowed above the house, disappearing with the breeze.

It was him. It was her father, Bernard Copperfield.

Julia's heart quickened with surprise. It was one thing to see the house and then another to see the man who'd destroyed their life there. She glared at him, remembering the last time she'd seen him in the flesh at the courthouse.

Th pipe was ridiculous. *Did he still think of himself as that pretentious, literary professor-type? Even after so many years locked away in prison?*

Then again, he'd paid his debt to society. Maybe that meant he was allowed a pipe puff here and there.

Annoyed, seething from a lifetime of rage, Julia stared up at him, daring him to look down at her. *What would he do when he saw her? That was a silly question, wasn't it?* Because actually, Julia was now a forty-two-year-old woman with three kids, a mortgage, a failing marriage, and a failing publishing house. She looked nothing like the whip-smart seventeen-year-old beauty she'd been when she'd skipped town.

Suddenly, his gaze dropped down to her. A shiver ran down Julia's spine. She locked eyes and waited as he lifted his pipe from his lips. After another pause, he raised a hand in greeting, then disappeared back in the window.

*Had he known it was her, his third child? Or had he just assumed she was a passing neighbor?*

There was no way to know. But Julia felt she'd traveled too far not to push herself all the way inside. *Think of your mother,* she told herself. *Think of all the trauma you caused.*

Julia squared her shoulders, regaining her confidence and headed for the front door. When the knob didn't turn, she checked under the nearest garden rock for the key and miraculously found it, right where it had probably lay for the previous twenty-five years. She eased the key into lock; the knob turned like putty in her hand.

The first thing Julia noticed was the smell of dust.

It was stuffy, shadowed, and dark even in the foyer, nothing like the illuminated and ever-clean-smelling place of her youth. In the old days, Greta had skittered in and out of the kitchen, demanding that whoever just came in taste-test the new recipe she'd concocted. You were normally full before dinner from all the taste-testing. As a teenager with an ever-present appetite, The Copperfield House was a version of paradise for Julia. Charlie, too, had reaped those rewards.

Charlie. His ruffled blonde curls. His supple lips and the

way he'd played Radiohead repeatedly, his eyes half-closed as he mouthed the words. She'd thought him to be the most creative and big-hearted creature on the planet. Julia had thought he would be her entire world. "As long as we have each other, we'll be all right."

The brain could play terrible tricks on you, couldn't it? Why, in the wake of her husband's decision to move to China, had her memories decided to bring out a slideshow of "best Charlie memories"? It was cruel.

"Hello?" Julia called out into the house, taking in the sight of the living room. In the corner, the old piano remained, crooked and untuned and heavy with dust. The same furniture remained in the room, save for a new television that caught the soft gray of the April sunlight.

"Hello?" Julia tried again, closing the door behind her. "Dad?"

How silly to say the word "*Dad*." She hadn't said it in twenty-five years, had she? She felt like she'd entered into a movie about someone else's life.

There was a groan in the next room. Julia walked toward the television and realized that there was a lump beneath a blanket on the nearby couch. A big rush of gray hair came out from under the blanket.

"Mom...?" Julia's throat tightened with fear. Although Greta Copperfield had already begun to gray before Julia's departure, she'd never once allowed her gray strands to show.

Not that it mattered, showing your age.

*Did it?* Julia had begun dying her hair at thirty-five and had never looked back. *Had it been societal pressure?* Maybe, or a comment Jackson had made once about her looking "a bit over her true age."

Julia hovered about six feet away from the figure beneath the blanket on the couch. A long time ago, a teenaged Henry had made her watch a horror movie, where the ghost had lifted from beneath a blanket and wafted across the room, screaming. *"Why do you watch this stuff, Henry?"* Julia had laughed at the time, her hands clasped tightly together as she'd watched with a mix of humor and fear.

The older woman who revealed herself from under the blanket blinked through the shadows of the room to find Julia there beside the piano, still dressed in her spring jacket. Although the woman wore a sleeping gown and no makeup, there was still a soft beauty to her— as though she was ethereal, otherworldly.

*Greta didn't recognize her. Or did she?*

"Mom?" Julia stepped toward Greta, dropping onto her knees beside the couch. "It's me. It's Julia." She reached beneath the blanket to take Greta's hand.

Still half asleep, Greta finally spoke, her voice so raspy that it was difficult to understand.

"He can't stay here. I can't take it. It's too much. He has to leave."

# Chapter Ten

"What about groceries? Someone must have seen someone dropping off the groceries."

"Not a soul."

"So, they've just seen his face outside the window? Smoking his pipe?"

"Apparently so."

"But what are they eating? How are they living? And what on earth does Greta think of him getting out of prison after all this time?"

"I would divorce him if I was her. Go off to New York City and live with that handsome son of hers, Quentin."

"Come on. You remember Quentin, don't you? He was such an arrogant guy. Awful to be around."

"I'd take an arrogant son any day, as long as he had the kind of cash to throw around that Quentin Copperfield has."

Charlie stood in his workshop with bated breath, listening to the gossip coming from the office. The gossiping parties included his secretary, Hannah, and a potential client, a local Nantucket woman who (twenty-five years ago) had previously dined at The Copperfield House joyously, chatting with Greta and swapping recipes. Charlie remembered seeing her there, a sort of overly-rich wicked witch type who'd married a man twice her age.

Now, she still had the money he'd left behind in death. That had been her plan, he supposed.

After the potential client left the shop, Charlie stepped into the foyer, swiping his hands across his thighs to remove the last of the wood shavings. He was hard at work on a commissioned wardrobe, one with intricate detail reminiscent of an antique French wardrobe he'd studied that had sold for five-thousand dollars. Imagining that his work might last one hundred, even two hundred years, often thrilled him. It was the only way to truly "live forever" through your work.

"What do you think about all this Copperfield stuff?" Hannah blinked up at him, a secretive smile across her lips.

Hannah was thirty years old, a family woman with a wholesome face and photographs of her children scattered across her desk. She'd probably been around four or five when Charlie and Julia had taken off for New York City, abandoning Nantucket and all they'd ever known for the adventure of a lifetime.

Hannah had no idea of Charlie's connection to the Copperfields. Charlie Bellows had grown up and grown older; he'd buried his beautiful wife, and his children had run off the island to build their own lives. Time was a great cavern, widening with each passing day.

"I'm not sure what to make of it myself," Hannah continued when Charlie offered no explanation. "My husband thinks that the rich men he stole from had it coming. And they've indeed kept on being just as rich since all that happened. They still have the same yachts and sailboats; they still own the most beautiful houses and take the most stunning European vacations."

Charlie cleared his throat as Hannah continued.

"All the while, Bernard Copperfield has lived in a prison cell in Upstate New York City. Can you imagine what he must feel like after all that time locked away?"

Charlie turned toward the coffee maker that sat in the corner, poured himself a cup, and stared out the window at the gray afternoon light. Hannah, accustomed to how quiet Charlie could be when he got lost in his head, had begun to type out an email to a client, humming to herself.

Suddenly, there was an alarming flash of red and blue lights out the window, followed by the whir of emergency vehicles. Charlie lay his coffee mug on the front desk and rushed out onto the street. He tried to calm himself down, to tell himself that everyone he'd ever really loved on the island no longer remained. But still, he watched, captivated, as the ambulance took a dramatic right turn, darting back toward the waterline—back toward The Copperfield House, which was only about a six-minute walk away.

"I'm going to take a walk," Charlie hollered back to Hannah. He then walked out into the afternoon chill, shoved his hands into his pockets, and quickly made his way toward that once-familiar street. Although he wasn't ordinarily a gossip fiend, an ache in his gut drew him deeper toward the sirens. He had to know.

Sure enough, when he turned down the Copperfield's old road, the ambulance flashed its red and blue lights directly before the old, haunted-looking Victorian home. Other neighbors stood out on their front porches or the well-manicured grass of their front lawns, watching with bated breath.

Here it was: the gossip they'd all talked about.

Finally, someone would be seen leaving The Copperfield House.

Charlie ran the rest of the way down the road, watching as one of the EMT workers burst out from the front door, easing a stretcher along with him. Another EMT worker jumped forward to open the ambulance's back door.

Charlie stopped short at the edge of the property, where the grass and weeds lifted high over the well-cut and nourished grass of the neighboring property. People were good about knowing where their property ended and another's began.

The stretcher drew closer, revealing an older woman with a wild frizz of gray hair as it billowed out around her head like a halo. *Was that Greta Copperfield, the woman who spoke three languages, wrote poetry, and could play any piano tune by heart?* Charlie's heart seized with sorrow at the sight, knowing full well that this was where time marched all of us.

And didn't he know it better than most? He'd carried his wife's coffin to its grave.

"Mom! Mom. I'm right here." A woman hustled out behind the stretcher, a willowy beauty with jet-black hair and almond-shaped eyes. She wore a black peacoat and a pair of skinny jeans, and there were mascara streaks down her cheeks, proof she'd been crying.

She was truly beautiful.

And she seemed completely out of context in this environment, there in front of the busted-out Victorian mansion, calling out for her mother.

Charlie's lips parted in surprise.

The woman before him was Julia Copperfield. It had to be. It was the first girl he'd ever loved.

"I have to come with you," Julia called to the EMT workers as they adjusted the stretcher in the back of the ambulance. "She can't go alone."

One of the EMT workers bent down to give Julia his hand. He then assisted her in, speaking something in lower tones that Charlie couldn't make out. Charlie hurried toward the driveway to stand behind the ambulance as the EMT workers began to close the double doors.

86

He locked his eyes on Julia, wide-eyed with shock.

He dared her to look up at him.

He dared her to see him, even in this terrible moment of shock.

But when her tear-filled eyes did lift toward his, time stood still just for a moment. Her lips parted with surprise, and her eyes shone with recognition. It was just like that last moment at the bus station in Greenwich Village twenty-five years ago. Since then, they'd lived a combined fifty years of happiness, sorrows, disappointments, and surprises. His heart ached to know every thought she'd had since that moment they'd parted ways.

He lifted a hand in greeting as her eyes swelled with shock.

And at that moment, the EMT workers shut the ambulance doors closed. It then drove out from the driveway, its sirens screaming as it made its way down the street. Charlie followed it until it disappeared out of sight. When he blinked himself back to reality, he realized that all of the neighbors, too, hovered at the edges of their driveways and turned toward the far end of the road.

"Was that Julia Copperfield?" one neighbor asked, loud enough for many other houses to hear him.

"I think it was," another called out.

"Where's Bernard in all of this?" another demanded.

Together, they turned toward The Copperfield House, scrutinizing its spurts of weeds, crooked shutters, and busted front porch. While his wife was rushed to the hospital, Bernard Copperfield remained within, lurking like a ghost. What on earth would happen next?

# Chapter Eleven

Julia hadn't been to the Nantucket Community Hospital since she'd broken her arm back in middle school. Back then, she'd sat gently weeping, her hand tenderly touching her wrist while her father read from *The Hobbit* as a way to distract her from her pain. They'd both adored the book, the fantastical descriptions and the poetics and whimsies of the characters. After Julia had gotten a cast on her wrist, her father had drawn a beautiful Hobbit-inspired illustration of a talking tree along it. Charlie had ached with jealousy for the drawing, wishing out loud that he'd been the one to break his wrist instead.

Speaking of Charlie...

*Had that been Charlie out on The Copperfield House drive-way, waving at her?*

It couldn't have been.

Could it?

Aged forty-two with a shattered heart and two intact wrists, Julia paced the waiting room with her hands latched tightly behind her back. She'd been told a doctor would come to speak to her soon, but "soon" felt like somewhere between five minutes and five hours, and she ached with worry.

How long had she been back on Nantucket? Two hours? Maybe three? And already, her mother was in the hospital, her father had remained in his Beauty-and-the-Beast-inspired "West Wing," and she'd struggled with the reality and state of her family's current situation.

The Copperfield House was borderline condemned. Her mother hadn't eaten anything in what seemed like days. And her father? Her father was a mystery, and maybe he always had been.

"Hello? Mrs. Copperfield?" A doctor in thick glasses stepped out from the back hallway.

"Crawford, actually. My married name is Crawford." Julia corrected him before she remembered she was on the verge of divorce. She joined him in the back hallway and crossed her arms tightly over her chest, worry mounting.

His face didn't look strained. Shouldn't he have at least pretended to be worried for the sake of her mother?

"Your mother has had a panic attack," the doctor said simply.

Julia shook her head, frustrated. "That wasn't a panic attack. It was more like a heart attack or a stroke."

"Sometimes, panic attacks can look like heart attacks," the doctor explained. He bowed his head and added, "Not to speak out of turn, but there's been a reasonable amount of added stress on Greta Copperfield in the previous week, hasn't there?"

Julia's throat tightened. She wanted to blare out just how stupid a question that was, but in actuality, what did she know about anything? She was a stranger.

"Yes, I guess it's no secret that my father just returned from prison," Julia replied.

"Has your mother been eating? Drinking water? Walking at all?"

"I'm not sure I can answer those questions. I just arrived from Chicago," Julia said, turning her eyes toward the ground. "I guess I came a little too late."

"As I said, it's just a panic attack brought on by stress and her lack of caring for herself properly," the doctor explained. "I'd like to hold her here overnight so that we can continue to give her fluids and help her get some much-needed rest. If she doesn't watch her stress levels and doesn't pay attention to her nutrition, she will have more trouble down the line. It's a sure thing. Do you understand me?"

Julia nodded, feeling like a child being scolded at school for not paying attention.

"Normally, parents struggle listening to their children. But you must stress the importance of this," the doctor added. "Greta is only seventy-one years old, and she should have plenty of years left."

A nurse led Julia to the room where Greta Copperfield now rested, her hands splayed softly across her chest and her eyelids glowing with the soft orange light from the overhead lamps. The sun had begun to set outside, casting a purplish light across the billowing clouds. Julia collapsed in the chair alongside her mother's hospital bed, too frightened to touch her.

The panic attack, or whatever it had been, had begun not long after Julia's arrival. Greta had gazed at her, aghast, as though she'd discovered a ghost lurking in the house. She'd then continued to mutter to herself about Bernard's return home and how he "never came down from up there" and how she could "smell his pipe smoke" and "wanted him gone for good."

"Mom, where else is he supposed to go?" Julia had finally asked her, already regretting her return to the nightmare.

"Don't you dare call me that."

"Call you what?" Julia had asked.

"Don't you dare call me 'Mom' as though you've been around all these years. You're no better than him, disappearing for twenty-five years." Greta had spat back.

Julia's stomach twisted at how her reappearance after twenty-five years away aggravated an already stressful time. And now, Greta Copperfield lay in a hospital bed, with a tube attached to her vein to deliver vital nutrients and fluids.

Julia dropped her chin to her chest, groaning inwardly. What did she think would happen after her abrupt drive from the Midwest? *Had she thought she could somehow unite Greta and Bernard again? Had she thought they'd catch up over clam chowder, that they'd give her solace after Jackson's abandonment — that they'd read poetry and sing songs and laugh till dawn?*

Perhaps she was more delusional than she thought.

As she sat in stunned silence, one of the doctor's sentences ran through her head.

"Parents struggle listening to their children."

Children, plural.

*Where were the other Copperfield children?*

*Alana? Ella?*

*And what about America's favorite morning showtime anchor, Quentin Copperfield? "The man Americans trust the most."*

Julia would have rather sawed off her arm than call Quentin Copperfield.

Ella had already dismissed her idea of returning, saying that she had problems of her own to deal with in New York City.

This left Alana.

It was currently six-fifteen in Nantucket, which meant that it was just past midnight in Paris. Julia scrambled through various social media accounts, hunting for Alana's phone number. Unlike Ella, Alana made herself much more available, still advertising herself as a "model and actress, available for projects big or small."

She'd also written this advertisement in French.

Julia headed into the hallway to make the call. The rings blared out across the Atlantic, probably buzzing through Alana's beauty sleep. Julia hadn't seen or spoken to Alana since the trial. Still, social media told her she was just as vain as ever, a true beauty of forty-four who'd ridden out the storyline of a twenty-something model and actress before ultimately riding the coattails of her famous painter husband's lifestyle.

Asher Tarkan— one of the most successful painters The Copperfield House had ever welcomed into their artist residency. His paintings now sold for upward of three-hundred-thousand dollars. Julia had read a review that referred to him as a modern-day Cy Twombly.

"Hello?" The voice on the other end of the line had the smallest Frenchified twinge, as though Alana had strained herself to rid her voice of her American accent.

"Hi, Alana." Julia had no idea how to begin. The woman on the other end was essentially a stranger. "It's um. It's Julia. Your sister."

"Julia?" Alana's voice buzzed with surprise. Unlike Ella, she sounded pleased to hear from her. "Well, isn't this something."

"Yes. I know it's late in Paris."

"Don't worry about that," Alana told her. "I'm actually on the Asian continent just now, watching the sunrise over the mountains."

Ah, yes. This was typical Alana, wanting to brag about the glamor of her everyday life.

"Sounds beautiful, Alana. Really."

"Well, anyway..." Alana remembered that this was her sister, whom she hadn't heard from in twenty-five years. "To what do I owe this pleasure, Julia? I don't suppose you and that handsome husband of yours are coming to Paris any time soon. We can't pretend that we haven't stalked one another on social media."

Tears threatened to crawl down Julia's cheek.

*Just say it,* Julia told herself. *Just speak the truth before it destroys you.*

"Actually, I'm calling from Nantucket."

The silence was deafening as Julia waited for Alana to respond.

"You went there..." Alana breathed finally. "I can't believe it. After all this time."

"I saw Dad on the news," Julia continued to explain. "And I couldn't just..."

"You wanted to see him? After all he did to us?" Alana demanded, sounding aghast. "You wanted to return to that house? You wanted to speak to the islanders who ridiculed us and made us feel two inches tall?"

"You don't understand, Alana." Julia continued.

"Don't you have a publishing house to run? A gorgeous husband? Three children?" Alana demanded. "Why on earth would you go back there after what we've all been through?"

Julia stuttered, unsure of how to proceed. She couldn't very well tell her estranged sister on the phone that her husband had left her and that her publishing house had failed. It revealed too much at once.

Instead, she said, "Mom is in the hospital and Dad won't leave his upstairs study. The house is falling into complete disrepair, and if someone doesn't step in to do something..."

"Then what, Julia? Tell me. What will happen if someone doesn't step in?" Alana demanded.

Julia dropped her head back against the painted bricks of the hospital hallway. *Why did she think Alana could see beyond herself?*

Or better yet, why had she assumed Alana would think that

Julia's return was "honorable" and "what they all should be doing"? All Julia had done was run from one batch of problems to another.

"You knew Nantucket was a mess," Alana continued to scold her. "It's your fault for going back." Alana had now lost all of the little bit of French accent she'd begun speaking with. After another moment of sizzling anger, she promptly hung up.

Julia stormed back into her mother's hospital room, where Greta continued to sleep peacefully. As she sat, crumpling in on herself, Julia prayed that Greta couldn't remember all the darkness out in the real world. She prayed that within her dreams, Greta knew only the beauty of the past— blissful afternoons beneath the Nantucket sun, with the promise of another night at The Copperfield House ahead.

# Chapter Twelve

D uring the particularly dark portions of Sally's cancer treatments and hospital visits, Charlie had had a little game, a deal he'd tried to make with the universe. "Maybe if I park in the furthest possible parking spot away from the front door, God will deem me a good and honorable person and keep my wife alive." It had been a ridiculous thought from a man on the brink of becoming a widower. And it hadn't worked.

When Charlie drove over to the hospital that evening, he parked closer to the front door than he ever had. These days, Charlie no longer believed in trying to make deals with the universe. He generally felt sure he lived in an uncaring universe that performed cruel actions despite how good or pure or honest you were. Truly horrific people had the best of circumstances, with plenty of love, money, and adventure, while funny, sweet, and adorable people like Sally were taken from the world at the young age of thirty-nine. You couldn't make sense of it, and it was better not to try.

Charlie entered the foyer of the hospital waiting room with

his hands shoved in his pockets. The woman at the front desk hadn't worked at the hospital during Sally's illness, but when she looked up to greet him, she greeted him by name. With a funny jolt, Charlie realized that he'd gone to high school with her— that she'd been in at least two or three classes with Julia and Charlie before they'd taken off for NYC.

"Charlie Bellows. It's good to see you."

Charlie willed himself to remember the woman's name but came up blank. He cursed his stupid, antisocial brain. He'd done little socializing in the past twenty-plus years, as he'd fallen deeply into the responsibilities of fatherhood, avoiding relationships with most other adults his age and using Sally as his all-purpose relationship: wife, best friend, lover, and companion.

The woman at the front desk bent her head knowingly and whispered, "I don't suppose you're here to see Julia?"

Charlie's throat tightened with surprise. It had been so long since anyone had remembered his relationship with Julia. They were inextricably linked after they abandoned the island and then the abandonment of each other.

"Is she still here?" he heard himself ask.

"I'm not supposed to give out information if you're not family," she simply told him.

"I understand," Charlie said hesitantly.

"But if the rumors are true, she's going to need a friend," the woman continued under her breath. She tore a sticky note from a big stack and wrote the number 417, which she slid across the counter toward him. "But again, I can't tell you where she is."

An alarm rang out through Charlie's skull. He took the paper and gave her a nod of understanding, not wanting to cause a scene with overzealous thanks. He then turned toward the elevator, his heart ramming against his ribcage.

Once in the elevator, he hit the fourth-floor button, then chickened out and got out on the second floor instead. Off to the right was a coffee shop, where he purchased a cappuccino and then an additional one for Julia. The paper cups burnt his hands, and he placed them timidly on an empty table and rubbed his palms together. *What the hell was he doing?*

He was going to see her.

The woman who'd told him not to come back to New York City.

The woman he'd left behind.

Did Julia remember that coffee shop they'd gone to in Greenwich Village, where they bought one-dollar cappuccinos and oatmeal cookies and read *The Village Voice* to each other until closing time? He certainly did. He remembered its freedom, the ease of those impossibly beautiful afternoons, and the feeling that they would never get those days back.

"I love you, Julia." He'd said it over the phone when she'd told him that it was time for them both to move on. "I don't know if I can."

"You'll be able to. You'll watch yourself move on, and you won't believe it at first. And then suddenly, you'll have this whole new life," she'd told him.

His heart had shattered when she'd said it. But he'd also known how right she was.

And, when he'd met and fallen in love with Sally, he'd half-thanked Julia for what she'd done. It had been the right thing. Maybe.

Armed with two cappuccinos and a heart on the verge of bursting, he returned to the elevator and buzzed to the fourth floor. The march to room 417 made his legs feel uneasy beneath him.

As he approached, a nurse stepped out of the room, whipping the door out wide to allow him a view of the small room within. Greta Copperfield was fast asleep, her thin skin pale in the soft light, and her lips parted slightly, as though she were a beautiful, older version of Snow White, awaiting her prince.

Besides the hospital bed, Julia Copperfield was wrapped up in a tight ball, her head splayed across the tops of her thighs. She stared forward, lost in thought.

Charlie stood as the door closed between them. He was just a foolish man with two cappuccinos and a lifetime of hurt, and he knew it was probably better for them both if he just returned home.

But before he could turn back, Julia sprung for the door and pushed it open. She stood, her lips parted and her beautiful eyes taking in the full breadth of him. *What could two ex-lovers possibly say to one another after so much time?*

"It's you," Julia finally breathed.

No one had looked at him like that in years, not until now, not until Julia's eyes locked onto his there at that moment.

He'd felt like a ghost in his own life, moving through it with hardly a thought.

"Would you like to go for a walk with me?" Charlie asked softly.

\* \* \*

Minutes later, Charlie and Julia stood at the edge of the parking lot, sipping their cappuccinos and watching as the last sunlight glittered over the tender expanse of green grass. They still hadn't said much more than, "How about we go outside?" and, "How is she doing?" and, "She's going to be all right. It looked a whole lot worse than it was. Thank goodness."

"This cappuccino is not bad," Julia said finally. "For hospital coffee." She sipped it again and added, "Thank you. I think I needed something like this, especially after the past few days of driving."

Charlie nodded. He felt like the most nervous, quivering creature on the planet. How could he translate how lonely he'd been? How could he tell her that standing there with her in a parking lot meant more to him than most things in his current existence?

"She had a panic attack," Julia finally confirmed. "But when it first started, I thought it was all over. That I'd been absent the last twenty-five years without speaking to any of them, only for my mother to die in front of me the minute I return."

"Gosh..."

"The guilt I feel right now is... not comfortable. But it's probably what I deserve."

Charlie shifted his weight. "I couldn't believe it when I saw you there, coming out of The Copperfield House like that."

"Why were you there?" Julia asked him, her voice barely a whisper.

"I heard the sirens, but to tell you the truth, I've avoided that house like my life depended on it for the past twenty-five years," he told her. "I wouldn't even take my kids trick-or-treating down that street, and I wouldn't glance at it when I was on the beach. But this week has been non-stop Copperfield gossip. And when I saw the ambulance heading that way... I just had to follow it."

Julia's eyes widened even as they shared the silence. The fact that he admitted he'd avoided her home was strange. Probably it had been too much. *How could anyone be sure of how much truth they were supposed to reveal? He was out of practice. He'd hardly ever told Sally the whole truth and nothing but the truth.*

"You must have come back because of Bernard?" he finally asked, wanting to draw the conversation back to facts.

Julia nodded. "I saw him on the news and couldn't believe it. A part of me knew that the twenty-five-year mark was approaching, but there was so much on my plate at home, and I managed to blot it out."

Julia lifted her left hand to slip a strand of hair behind her ear. Her wedding ring flashed menacingly.

"Your family has been a mystery since everything happened," Charlie offered. "Your mother was smart not to offer any additional gossip. You know that the island would have taken anything she said to them and ran with it."

"Yes, but that means she's just been alone by herself in that big house all this time," Julia whispered. "I don't know how I'll ever forgive myself for that."

Charlie nodded. He, too, lifted his left hand to brush a leaf from his jacket sleeve, not realizing that he flashed his wedding band, just as Julia had. Julia's eye caught the band, and she nodded tenderly.

"Gosh, so much time has passed, hasn't it?" Her cheeks looked bloody with embarrassment and sorrow.

"You're telling me," he said.

Julia cleared her throat. "But it looks like everything worked out well for you."

Charlie cocked his head. Perhaps he'd assumed that she knew about Sally's death and about his daughters leaving the island for university. But how could she have known? He didn't put anything on social media, as that had been Sally's thing. He didn't share his thoughts with anyone.

"I'm glad it all worked out for you, too," Charlie told her simply, not wanting to get into it.

After all, this woman was basically a stranger.

Julia lifted her cappuccino and cleared her throat. "Thanks again for this. I need to get back in there, just in case she wakes up."

"Of course. I just wanted to check-in and make sure you were okay," Charlie said.

"I am. I mean, I will be." Julia tried on a smile that promptly fell from her face. "Maybe we can catch up later this week before I head back to Chicago."

"Yeah. Maybe."

Julia turned on her heel and rushed headlong toward the hospital door, which burst open to swallow her back inside. Charlie continued to hold onto his cappuccino until she disappeared, then he threw it into the nearest trash can, overwhelmed with anger at himself, at his life.

People didn't just rekindle friendships with their high school sweethearts.

Especially not people like him, sad widowers without a single friend to call their own.

"It was good you tried it," he told himself as he hunted through his pocket for his keys. "But no more trying for a little while. You know that you're better off alone."

# Chapter Thirteen

After visiting hours ended that evening, Julia called a driving service to pick her up from the front of the hospital. A harsh wind erupted from the Atlantic, making her knees clack together with a chill as she waited, analyzing the plate numbers of the cars approaching. It had been one hell of a day, a day for the ages, and she wanted nothing more than to collapse at a local hotel, drink an entire bottle of wine, and prepare mentally and emotionally for the days ahead.

Once buckled in the back of the car, Julia sent a text message to Ella.

**JULIA: I just wanted to let you know that Mom is in the hospital due to a panic attack.**

She gave Ella no other information, feeling resentful and childish, like a teenage girl. Instead, she shoved her phone deep into her purse, dropped her head on the headrest, and listened to the talk radio station that purred around her. In this particular radio broadcast, people called in from coast-to-coast to talk about the loves they'd lost, the loves they still thought about, and the people who'd changed their lives forever. It was sappy, but in the wake of Charlie's sudden appearance, it crackled the edges of Julia's heart. She had a thing or two to say about Charlie Bellows, about what had happened between them and the strange love she'd felt when she'd seen him, as though it had been hibernating within her all that time.

The car dropped her off at the grocery store downtown just as she'd asked. Exhausted and a little annoyed, she made her way into the grocery store, nearly toppling over a large selection of Tostitos chips in flavors like lime and chili. Julia shoved the lime one in a basket, then made her way through the cheeses, the fruits, and the vegetables. She paused to grab fresh pasta, then selected three bottles of wine. In a previous version of her life, she'd spent more than two hundred dollars in groceries per week to support a family of five. Did this suit her plan to sit around in a hotel room and regret what had become of her life? It didn't.

But already, she recognized that she had a very different plan.

She was headed back to The Copperfield House, wasn't she?

She couldn't stand that Bernard Copperfield lurked in the upstairs study alone.

She couldn't stand that he waited up there, smoking his pipe and not even bothering to come down during his wife's health emergency.

He'd cultivated her teenage rage years ago, and now it was time to stomp up to him and demand why he'd done what he'd done. He couldn't get away with lurking in that study alone, and he couldn't get away with destroying their family.

But mid-way through the wine aisle, Julia lifted her head to find two pairs of eyes watching her.

The couple before here were in their late sixties, smartly dressed, the woman still with dark hair due to a dye job and the man sporty, with broad shoulders from his many years of sailing across the ocean.

Julia would have recognized them anywhere. They were Gregory and Bethany Puck, and they'd been dear friends of her parents back in the day. She'd watched them eat, drink, and laugh alongside her parents during the first seventeen years of her life— all before Gregory had been one of the men who'd accused Bernard of stealing more than six million dollars from him.

Julia knew she'd given the game away. She'd stared too long, revealing herself.

"Julia? Is that Julia Copperfield?" Bethany gasped.

"Why yes. I believe it is. And look at how she looks at us? Like we're ghosts?" Gregory said.

Julia's stomach curdled with anger. She dropped another bottle of wine into her grocery basket and glared at him, at this man who'd sat on the stand and destroyed her family forever.

Silence swelled between the three of them. Julia wanted to make this just as uncomfortable for them as it was for her, but she wasn't sure she knew exactly how to do that.

"I suppose you've been hanging around your father after his release?" Gregory accused, his words slimy. "Welcoming him back to reality?"

Julia flared her nostrils angrily. *What could she possibly say to this horrible man?*

"Gosh, I think about those last few months..." Gregory continued seedily. "Him hanging around with that little blonde bimbo of his. What was her name again? Megan? Mallory?"

"Marcia," Bethany corrected.

Julia had hardly thought of Marcia Conrad in years, the young filmmaker and writer who'd last idealized her father before running off to Los Angeles.

"Gosh, she seemed like such a prop for him, didn't she?" Gregory continued. "While he stole my money right out from under me, she was always right there, performing for us and distracting us from what he was up to."

"She was just as arrogant as all of the writers at that house, but you boys were so distracted by how she looked," Bethany teased.

Gregory cast his wife a sharp look, one that snapped Bethany's lips shut. Julia's anger rose like a wave within her, pouring across her heart.

"You tell that father of yours that I'll be waiting for him," Gregory spat, his voice sharp-edged.

Julia lifted her chin, surprising herself. "Mr. Puck, my father paid his debts to society. He spent twenty-five years in prison. Not only has he not eaten a single five-course meal in twenty-five years, but he also hasn't met a single one of his grandchildren or gone for a walk in the woods or kissed his wife during that time."

Julia's volatility affected both Gregory and Bethany, who remained silent as she continued.

"You both know how much he loved my mother," Julia blared, almost embarrassing herself now. "It was unquestioned, so I suggest you keep your mouth shut with your false accusations."

Julia then turned on her heel and stormed away from Gregory and Bethany, enraged and headed straight for the cashier at the exit. She paid with the credit card that read "Julia Crawford" and seethed. She was thousands of miles away from any concept of life she understood— and yet she was only about a half-mile from home.

Ignoring her plan to collapse at the nearest hotel, Julia carried her groceries back to The Copperfield House, where she let herself in through the still-open door. The kitchen light remained on, glowing off to the left. It was reminiscent of another time when the family had gathered to sing, and gossip as the skillets sizzled with dinner.

"Hello?" she called, surprising herself.

Julia's paper bags ruffled as she approached the kitchen. From the doorway, she peered over to find an old man bent over a glass of dark red wine, his white hair curling around his ears. He wore a thick pair of wool socks and flannel pajama pants, and his t-shirt illustrated a Led Zeppelin tour poster from forty-five years ago.

It was Bernard Copperfield.

A strange itch in the back of Julia's mind told her to hug him and tell him how much she'd missed him.

But instead, she held herself back and waited for him to turn around and greet her. It was his duty to do that, wasn't it? She'd driven across half of the continent to stand there, and all he'd done was get released from prison.

When he spoke, Bernard Copperfield talked mostly to the glass of wine before him rather than toward his daughter.

"I was asleep when I heard the sirens."

Julia's heart leaped into her throat. His voice was deep and masculine yet still slightly musical, like it had always been when he'd been particularly excited about something. It was strange to hear it again, and it transported her back to her youth.

"By the time I ran downstairs to figure out what was wrong, the ambulance was leaving the driveway. I couldn't believe it."

Julia stepped toward the counter, where she placed the bag of groceries. She then grabbed a wine glass from the cabinet, washed the dust off, and sat across from her father. He still refused to look at her, as though her eyes were powerful black holes, threatening to suck him up.

After a long, horrible pause, Julia finally spoke.

"She's okay, and they're keeping her overnight to get her levels up. But it wasn't anything really serious."

Bernard's shoulders dropped forward with relief. He took a

long sip of his wine as Julia filled her glass from his bottle. Julia took a sip, allowing the dry red to coat her tongue.

There was so much she wanted to ask him. Most of those questions, she didn't want the answer to. His cheeks hung sadly, drooping, and the corners of his eyes illustrated his dramatic, older age. Twenty-five years in prison. What did that even mean?

"I know I've put her through so much. More than any woman should ever go through," Bernard said finally, his eyes trained toward the table. "I promised to love her through all the days of my life. And instead..." He shook his head and took another sip.

"She's going to be okay," Julia murmured.

"I don't know. I don't know if any of us will be okay." Bernard cleared his throat. "When I saw you out on the street, I asked myself... Why did she come all this way just to fall back into my mess?"

Julia's lips parted in surprise. Her father was just an old man now. An old man who'd paid for his mistakes in one of the worst possible ways. This man didn't know anything about her beyond her seventeenth year.

"Look at this place, Dad." Julia began tenderly. "It's falling apart."

Bernard shook his head, eyeing the table.

"I think we should make an effort and restore it to what it was before. I think it could help Mom."

Bernard grunted, sipped his wine, then said, "Too much time has passed. It's clear to me, now."

Julia's lips parted in surprise. "Too much time has passed to put the house back together again? What does that mean? Is it supposed to just stand here and rot for the rest of time?"

Bernard's eyes illuminated several emotions: anger and sorrow, and fear.

And finally, he breathed, "I think it would be better for us if we just burned The Copperfield House to the ground."

Julia gaped at him, aghast. She'd never heard a more selfish sentiment. All those years, his wife had stayed on at The Copperfield House, becoming its ghost, while her husband paid his debt to society, rotting away in some jail cell.

"Are you kidding me?" she shot, her voice rising a few octaves. Julia grabbed her glass of wine and stormed toward the door between the kitchen and the living room, overwhelmed with fatigue and emotion.

"There's nothing for any of us here," Bernard grunted, mostly to himself. "It would be the best."

"If you're just going to give up on your life like this, why don't you just go back to prison?" Julia demanded.

She then stormed up the staircase toward the bedroom she'd abandoned all those years ago.

# Chapter Fourteen

The bedroom Julia had left twenty-five years ago remained nearly intact. A museum preserved to memorialize Julia Copperfield— the girl she'd been and the woman she'd wanted to be. Poetry books lined the bookshelves, many of which were underlined and noted with her emotions and feelings. Paintings she'd finished in high school hung crooked on the walls, including one of Charlie Bellows, his dark blonde hair ruffling through the wind as they walked the woods. She remembered the old photograph that she'd taken the image from, remembered the long-ago day when she'd taken it as they'd meandered together, lost in love and conversation. The photograph had probably been lost to time.

Lucky for Julia, someone, maybe Greta herself, had recently dusted the place, and the closet revealed a pile of clean sheets and pillowcases, which Julia dressed the bed with. Julia remembered what Ella had said about her children and how Greta had helped with babysitting them when Ella and Will went on tour. Perhaps they'd been here a time or two, sleeping in the creaky old Copperfield House and scampering down the sands of Steps Beach. After her departure, the Copperfield House had had some sort of life, but it was difficult to feel it, especially with all her things lying in wait for her.

Julia slept fitfully that night, tossing and turning beneath the comforter as her mind turned like an old washing machine. Around midnight, Rachel, her youngest, texted to say she struggled with her French assignment and wondered if her mother could check over her essay, which was due at the end of the week. Julia blinked at the text, genuinely surprised that Rachel had been able to contact her at The Copperfield House. No, her children didn't know where she was and assumed she remained in Bartlett, helping Jackson pack up for his adventure in Beijing. But that was the thing about cell phones. You could be anywhere, doing anything— and people could just reach out and contact you. It seemed strange, especially sleeping so close to the landline she'd used as a teenage girl.

**JULIA: Of course, honey. Send everything to my email, and I'll look it over.**

**JULIA: How are you doing otherwise?**

**RACHEL: Not bad! I keep thinking about China. It'll be so exciting for all of us to visit him.**

**RACHEL: Do you think you'll try to spend part of the year there to be with Dad?**

Julia's heart seized. She shoved her phone beneath her pillow, pressed her head deeper into its jagged corners, and pretended that she hadn't read the message. Was the question a trap to get Julia to admit that she and Jackson were through? Or did her children think that Julia and Jackson's love could last while he was so far across the Pacific Ocean?

Around six in the morning, a bang erupted downstairs and yanked Julia from her sleep. She grabbed her phone and hustled through the darkness, scrambling for the light switch. It took a couple of seconds for her to come to terms with where she was. As her stomach twisted with a mix of yesterday's left-over emotions, another crash came from downstairs, followed by a wild, "Shhh."

Julia stepped gingerly into the hallway, turning off the light in the bedroom and bringing her cell phone to her chest. She was prepared to hide in the upstairs closet and call the police at a moment's notice. She was reminded of thrillers and crime shows where the silly women went off to "investigate" a noise, only to wind up dead a few minutes later—*murdered in The Copperfield House!* That would have been quite a story.

"Honey, just set your bags down." A woman's voice came from downstairs, exasperated and lined with exhaustion.

"Mom, you should sit." This was a teenage boy, clearly worried. "You just drove five hours in the middle of the night."

"I know, honey. You both must think I'm crazy."

Julia's stomach twisted with the realization that the woman downstairs, the "mother," was her sister, Ella. She rushed for the staircase, swirling down its circular form until she burst into the foyer to find the three of them— Ella and her teenage children, all with dark hair, leather jackets, and half-opened eyes. You could tell they lived in the city, so unlike the sparkle of the suburbs Julia had grown to know so well.

And Ella, who was only about fifteen months younger than Julia, still looked to be in her mid-thirties, as though her decision to be in an indie rock band through her twenties, thirties, and now early forties had brought her a permanent feeling of "youth."

Well, that and the leather jacket seemed to be putting in a lot of work to give her that appearance.

For a long moment, Ella and Julia peered at one another, eyes enormous, both in different phases of exhaustion. Julia hadn't seen Ella since around the time of Bernard's sentencing and hadn't even stuck around to say goodbye that fateful day when she and Charlie had decided to run away.

"Ella..." Julia finally spoke first, her shoulders falling

forward. She wanted to throw her arms around her sister, weep, yell, and tell her how much her heart had missed her over the past twenty-five years. But instead, she said, "You got my text."

Ella's nostrils flared as she leafed through her pocket and drew out her cell. She read the text aloud with a harsh tone.

*"Just wanted to let you know that Mom is in the hospital due to a panic attack."* Ella looked enraged. "What kind of message is that, Julia? I didn't even see it till I got out of band practice at around eleven-thirty. I gathered the kids up and drove us down here immediately."

Julia dropped her gaze to the hardwood floor. "I'm sorry about that. I sent the text without thinking. It was a terrible day. Just terrible."

Ella's face smoothed slightly as she took in the news. Finally, she whispered, "I honestly can't believe you're here."

Finally, the girls flung forward and hugged, giving in to their impulses and bleeding hearts. Julia shivered against her sister, then lifted her head, blinking back the tears in her eyes. She rubbed the leather of her sister's jacket, feeling the tension in her shoulders.

"I can't believe you drove all night," she said finally.

Ella shrugged. "I couldn't get what I said the other night out of my head about this being your mission, not mine. It sounded so selfish. This is my home. My family. What kind of person am I if I turn my back on it now, when my sister finally wants to give it a chance?"

Shame curled around in Julia's stomach and planted itself there. *She'd been the one to turn her back on her family during its darkest hour? But it didn't seem like Ella wanted to point fingers or swing around blame.*

Instead, Ella said, "Do you know if there's any coffee?"

Julia led her sister and her teenagers into the kitchen, where they sat, still in their leather jackets, and watched silently as Julia prepared a big pot of coffee. The teenagers seemed to have a secret language with one another, one that required no verbal words.

When Julia placed a mug in front of the girl, the girl thanked her, took the cup, and said, "So you're my Aunt Julia? I've heard about you. About your publishing house out in Chicago. I'm a big reader, and I love to write. Mom said I always reminded her of you."

Julia's heart filled with immediate love for this beautiful young woman, whose name, she learned shortly after, was Laura. The boy introduced himself as Danny. Both seemed intelligent and interested, confident in ways only city kids were confident. Julia brushed her fingers through her wild black hair, nervous she looked out of sorts in front of these trendy New Yorkers.

"You told them I own a publishing house?" Julia asked Ella timidly, pouring another mug of coffee.

"I think Mom probably told them first," Ella admitted.

"Right, because she comes into the city." Julia finished.

"And we've been here a few times," Laura added. "At The Copperfield House."

"Sometimes, if the tour went on too long in the summertime, we dropped them off here," Ella explained, both hands wrapped tightly around her mug. "It's probably been five or six years since then. The place has fallen apart even more."

"Looks haunted," Danny added.

"You should have seen it back in the day," Julia said, surprising herself with her nostalgia. "Artists and writers from all over the world, coming in and out. Your grandmother cooking gorgeous French meals all the time. The hardwood glowed as though it was a house made in heaven itself."

"Here she goes. Writer Julia..." Ella teased, giving Julia a half-smile.

Julia's lips parted with surprise. "I must be delusional this morning. I apologize."

"No way. Don't apologize on our account. We're just as loopy as you are, maybe more," Ella told her. She sipped her coffee, clicking her nail against the mug. "How is Mom doing?"

Julia launched into an explanation about the previous day's events, how their mother hadn't eaten anything in days, how she wanted Bernard gone immediately, and how Julia had thought she had a heart attack. Still, it had just turned out to be a panic attack. Ella listened in stunned silence as the teenagers continued with their non-verbal communication, illustrating their shock.

"I ran into one of Dad's old friends at the grocery store. Gregory Puck. He made me so angry," Julia continued, adding just a dollop of milk into her mug. "I never thought in a million years that I would stand up for Dad, but when Gregory started digging into me in the wine aisle, I said something like, 'He's paid his debt to society!' I probably sounded insane."

"It's true, though," Laura offered simply.

"It is. But gosh, it's so complicated." Ella returned to her daughter.

"I don't know. I think people should be forgiven, especially if they've paid for their crimes," Laura said, as simple as anything.

Ella and Julia locked eyes at this explanation, genuinely surprised at the lucidity of this young woman. Granted, she'd never met Bernard Copperfield and hadn't been in existence when the events of 1996 and 1997 had taken place.

But still, what she said made some sense.

Julia went on to talk about their father at the kitchen table, telling them that he'd taken to his study and refused to come down.

"I don't think he accepts how old he is or what he's missed over the years," Julia stated sadly. "Mom's like a stranger to him."

"I can't imagine what they think of each other after all this time," Ella said. "Gosh, remember how in love they seemed back in the day?"

Julia nodded, allowing herself the images of those memories, even though they seemed so meaningless now.

"It's weird to talk about him now that he's just upstairs," Ella breathed a few moments later, her eyes toward the ceiling.

"I can't imagine he's getting much sleep," Julia said.

Julia poured them another round of coffee and then began to make toast, a great big pile of it, which the teenagers ate quickly, as though it was nothing at all. Julia remembered this from the recent days of having her teenagers around.

"I wish you could meet my children, or rather your cousins," she told them simply. "Rachel's nineteen, Henry's twenty, and Anna's twenty-two."

"You were so young when they were born," Ella commented. "All the way out in the Midwest... And that was so soon after you and Char—"

Julia didn't want to talk about her running away with Charlie, not this early and not in front of the niece and nephew she'd only just met.

"Yeah, but you do what you have to do when you have young children, don't you?" Julia said instead, interrupting.

"Of course," Ella replied with a sigh. "You just make things work. It's all it is."

A little while later, when the teenagers began to slow their roll on the toast pile, Julia announced that visiting hours began at the hospital at ten. "I think Mom will be thrilled to see all of us there."

"You got that right," Ella said. "But in the meantime... I think we should start cleaning this place up. Make it livable for all of us. The kids have spring break right now, and we need a break from the city, anyway."

Over the next three hours, Julia, Ella, Danny, and Laura began to attack the dusty old place, clearing out broken items, sweeping and mopping and removing cobwebs. Bit by bit, The Copperfield house began to reveal itself to them, coming back from the dead.

With Danny and Laura in the kitchen brewing another pot of coffee, Julia and Ella entered one of the other studies located downstairs. In this space, many of the writers from the residency had congregated to talk about their current manuscripts and ask their father for writing advice. The place was a pigsty of countless manuscripts and old, dusty books— a shrine to a forgotten era of writing. Six copies of their father's world-famous book, What They Knew, lined the top bookshelf, untouched.

"He always kept these around to give out to people at the residency," Ella noted with a sad laugh, grabbing one and looking at the cover. "Did you ever read it?"

"No, I never did. It's over one thousand pages," Julia pointed out. "I didn't have the time back then and won't make the time now."

"Yeah, well. You heard that the book was optioned for a film, right? It's how Mom managed to pay back so much of the money Dad stole. And it's also how she managed to live out the past twenty-five years. I'm sure most of the money is gone by now with just pennies left over."

"Gosh, I never knew... Did they ever make the movie?"

"They did. It hardly appeared in any cinemas in the United States and had more of a following in Europe," Ella explained.

"That's so Dad, isn't it? Always finding his niche audience somewhere."

Julia and Ella laughed as they returned to one of the large desks located in front of one of the larger bay windows that offered a beautiful view of the beach just beyond. A stack of manuscripts in the corner of the desk was left-over from the last residents that had come to stay at The Copperfield House during the autumn of 1996.

Julia leafed through the manuscripts, remembering the cast of characters from that last autumn— the filmmakers, the writers, and the guy who always carried around a guitar.

"Did any of these people ever become anything at all?" Ella asked, eyeing the manuscript stack.

"I don't know. It would be nice if they did, though, right?" Julia asked before laughing and adding, "I spoke too soon. I'm standing in front of indie rock royalty."

"Yeah, like that means anything," Ella quipped. "There's no money in indie rock. Our middling success in the 'oos wasn't enough to keep the rent paid this long, anyway. Will has a full-time job, and I work part-time gigs here and there to make ends meet. Tour is profitable, and we have great fans across the continent... but it's not always feasible, especially because we decided to have kids. Oh, and there's the fact that we're old now, and we don't exactly love being out on the road."

Julia nodded, grateful for Ella's honesty. "It looked like a blast while it lasted, though."

"It was..." Ella replied wistfully.

One of the final manuscripts in the pile had been written by Marcia Conrad, which jolted Julia's memory from the evening before. "Gregory Puck brought her up with me at the grocery store!" she exclaimed, shaking her head at the old manuscript. "Everyone said that Dad was having an affair with her."

"Do you believe it?" Ella asked, cocking an eyebrow.

"I don't know, and I don't want to believe it. But I didn't want to believe that Dad did what he did to his best friends and colleagues. Staring the truth in the face is the best way to go. At least then, you can move forward with your life."

# Chapter Fifteen

By the time nine-thirty a.m. chimed on the ancient grandfather clock in the living room, both Danny and Laura were stretched out on two of the living room couches, twitching in their sleep. Ella and Julia discovered them when they stepped out of the study and gave a wry laugh.

"I guess they ate too much toast," Julia offered.

"It's my fault. I kept them awake all night long to get here," Ella said. "I would wake them up, but I'm terrified of grumpy teenagers."

"Yeah. We have enough problems without that kind of attitude," Julia joked.

Julia and Ella took quick showers and met in the foyer a little after ten. Julia jangled her keys from her spring jacket and led Ella wordlessly to her SUV, where it remained stationed at the side of the road. Ella's station wagon, which was parked directly in the driveway, was clunky and vintage-looking, like a prop for a seasoned New York artist. By contrast, Julia's SUV was fit for a soccer mom. If only she still had someone to drive to soccer.

"Wow. Heated seats?" Ella hissed excitedly a minute or so after Julia turned on the engine.

"It got so cold in Bartlett," Julia explained. "When I was driving Henry to basketball, Anna to play practice, and Rachel to gymnastics, I spent a lot of time in this car."

"On top of your publishing house in the city?" Ella asked.

"For a while, I felt like I had two lives," Julia told her. "I wanted to perform all the duties of Super Mom, and I wanted to be a top-grade businesswoman. I probably failed at both."

"It doesn't look like you did. Not from here on your heated seats."

They drove the rest of the way to the hospital in silence. The clock next to the speaker system told her the date— April 7th. *When was Jackson taking off for Beijing? Was it April 8th? Sometime that weekend?* As she'd once known the ins and outs of everything from Jackson's writing schedule to his underwear drawer, her heart yearned to know the intricacies of his schedule. That feeling wouldn't go away quickly. She knew that.

Once in the hospital's foyer, the smell of sterilization equipment and bad hospital food wafted through the room. Julia's stomach twisted with fear. The woman at the front desk greeted them as they checked in, saying, "I don't know the last time I saw so many Copperfields at once."

Julia and Ella glanced at one another, simmering with the same feeling: *Haven't you people learned to just leave us alone? Haven't we been your sideshow long enough?*

Julia and Ella took the steps to Room 417. The door was propped open, and sunlight brewed out from the large window, drawing a halo around the doorframe and into the hallway. Julia watched as Ella stepped into the hospital room first, her hands clasped tightly behind her back.

"Is that my Ella?" Greta Copperfield's voice was twice as bright as the day before, flowing with happiness.

"Mom..." Ella rushed to the bedside as Julia stepped in to join them. She paused in the doorway, leaning against the frame as Ella dropped low to kiss their mother on the cheek lovingly. Her leather jacket played out such a contrast to the sterile white of the hospital room and the beeping machines. Greta Copperfield didn't seem to care.

"Oh, Ella, my darling. I hope you didn't leave anything important behind to come here just for little old me," Greta told her as Ella stepped back, drawing her fingers through her mother's.

Ella turned to catch Julia's eye. Hers glittered with a mix of fear and love, a love for where they'd come from and who they'd once been. Greta followed Ella's gaze to catch Julia in the doorway, feeling like a stranger.

"You came together?" Greta's eyes widened with surprise as she took in the gorgeous sight of these two women, her children— only one of whom had maintained ties with her. Only one of whom had called her on her birthday.

Julia stirred with resentment toward that previous version of herself, the one who'd burned every bridge.

"Julia..." Greta shook her head tenderly, reaching out her other hand.

The gesture was so pure, a mother yearning so desperately to hold onto as many of her children as possible. Julia recognized this feeling within herself when she forced herself not to text her children too much for fear they'd think she was needy or weak.

There they sat: Julia on one side, Ella on the other, and Greta in the middle, holding her two youngest daughters' hands. Her eyes were damp with tears.

"I don't quite know what to say," Greta finally said. "Last night, I had a dream about you, Julia. You were just a little girl, and we were running across the beaches of Nantucket, singing songs and rushing through the waves. I woke up with the strangest feeling that I'd seen you just recently. And now, here you are."

"She was with you yesterday, Mom," Ella told her softly. "It's why I knew you were in the hospital in the first place."

Greta's face shone with disbelief. After another strange and pregnant pause, she whispered, "Well, I'll be," because really, there was nothing else to do but marvel at the beauty of this reunion.

The door creaked to reveal the doctor from the previous evening, who reported that Greta's vital signs were promising and that she could even return home that afternoon. Greta's face twisted with a wave of fear, to which Julia whispered, "We've made the house look really nice, Mom. And Dad won't bother you. We'll figure something out."

"You need to make sure her stress levels are low," the doctor told them pointedly. "And that she eats three meals a day plus snacks." He then turned his gaze toward Greta, like a stern teacher, to say, "You hear that, Mrs. Copperfield? You're significantly underweight. You better let your daughters here take you out for ice cream."

Julia and Ella caught one another's gaze for a long moment as Greta shivered ominously between them. There was something strange about a doctor speaking "down" to their mother in this way, as though she was a child without the mental capacity to understand.

"We've got this," Julia told the doctor with finality, using that business-world voice she'd cultivated over her decades in the publishing world.

\* \* \*

Julia and Ella had brought a pair of clothes for Greta: some slacks and a black turtleneck, plus socks, underwear, a bra, and a pair of tennis shoes, which had still been in the box they'd been delivered in. Greta remained a regal and proud woman and refused to let herself be dressed. Julia and Ella turned around to give her privacy as she shimmied into her pants.

"These tennis shoes don't quite match the rest of the ensemble you girls packed for me," Greta said.

"We wanted you to have the support to walk around, Mom," Ella said coaxingly.

"Support comes long after fashion," Greta returned, evoking a much younger version of herself.

"We can throw them into the ocean after we get home," Julia quipped. "Let's just get you home safe."

A nurse arrived with the wheelchair Greta was required to depart the hospital in. Julia signed several pieces of paperwork and then followed along with Ella as she pushed her mother toward the elevator and the double-wide doors on the ground floor. The three Copperfield women were silent, too afraid to speak as they worked their way toward the illumination of this glorious April day.

Once outside, Greta lifted herself onto her tennis shoes timidly. Julia stepped toward her to draw a hand across her back for support. Greta turned her eyes toward her, giving her a once over.

"You were always so beautiful, Julia. And now, at forty-two years old, you evoke a similar beauty to my mother." Greta's voice cracked as she said it, overwhelmed with the sight of the girl who'd left her behind.

Ella zipped her leather jacket as Julia struggled to know what to say next. It was alarming that her mother knew her exact age, as though she'd celebrated each and every birthday without her. Julia could envision herself doing the same with her children, thinking of the unique birth stories of Anna,

Henry, and Rachel and her very unique love for each of them.

"I think we should go out for lunch," Ella suggested, looking from her mother to her sister.

"Go out?" Greta asked, as though it was the most outrageous concept she'd ever heard of.

"That's a great idea," Julia countered.

"It's just..." Greta stumbled over her words as they moved deeper through the parking lot. "I just don't..."

"You've been hiding from all the nosy islanders of Nantucket for too long, Mom," Ella told her. "And even though I want to have a word with how disrespectful that doctor acted back there, his point about going out and eating a lot was a good one. Why don't we go to that restaurant you always loved?"

"The French café!" Julia cried, her heart lifting with the joy of a thousand beautiful memories with their mother at Chez Longue. Chez Longue was a delectable little French restaurant that sold a wide array of crepes, sandwiches, omelets, cheese platters, and other French delicacies along the water's edge.

Julia parked the SUV outside the cottage, with its slanted rooftops and white-painted porch overlooking the water. A crooked sign above the doorway read: CHEZ LONGUE, and a sign out front illustrated a wide array of specials for the afternoon ahead.

"Remember when you had your book club here?" Julia said suddenly as the memory rushed through her. "We would come here after school and listen to you talk about the books you'd read."

Greta's eyes lit up with the joint memory. "I loved leading that little group. We read some fantastic things together. *The Sound and the Fury* by William Faulkner. *One Hundred Years of Solitude* by Gabriel Garcia Marquez."

"Do you still read often?" Julia asked her mother.

Greta shook her head timidly; her grey curls flashed around

her ears. "I feel that I haven't had a concrete thought in over ten years."

A server in her early twenties showed the three Copperfield women to the corner table, which offered a gorgeous view of the Brant Point Lighthouse. The server poured them sparkling water into three water glasses as they studied the menus, all wordless as they took in the dynamic flavor pairings and listened to the rush of the waves outside. Occasionally, Greta's eyes flashed up and around her as though she dared anyone to approach, to ask her how she was.

Julia supposed that she would have stayed locked away in The Copperfield House all these years, too. The embarrassment of being the wife of the island criminal was too much to bear.

Eventually, Julia ordered for them: a charcuterie board filled with various cheeses, croissants, jams, dips, a large bowl of olives, smoked salmon, and a crepe with goat cheese and honey to share. To drink, they ordered tea, too fearful that coffee would push Greta's heart over the edge again.

"No stress," Ella repeated sweetly as they piled the menus together and passed them back to the server.

As they sipped tea and waited for their food to arrive, the conversation shifted evenly toward what Ella and Greta knew about one another, leaving Julia on the sidelines.

"Tell me about Danny and Laura," Greta said, sighing. "I haven't seen them in so long. It has to be at least two summers now. Time seems to pass by quickly, especially when you get to my age."

"They're actually back at The Copperfield House," Ella told her. "Sleeping in the living room."

Greta's face twisted. "I hope your father doesn't come downstairs and scare them. What a shock that would be."

"My kids are tough," Ella told her simply. She then turned

her eyes toward Julia's as she added, "I imagine yours are, as well. All out of the house now, right?"

Julia recognized this as an olive branch. Ella wanted to bring Julia into the conversation, to shed light on the world Julia had created for herself back in Chicago. Greta's eyes illuminated with excitement.

"Julia... Your children. Tell me about them."

This was a topic Julia could speak about for hours. She leafed for her phone and flashed through the images: Rachel at her recent high school graduation, Henry at an intellectual competition for the University of Chicago, and Anna on the day they'd dropped her off in Seattle for her internship. Greta held the phone with both hands, beaming with pride at the images of these beautiful young adults, the grandchildren she'd never been allowed to meet.

Julia heard herself say, "I know they'd love to meet their grandmother."

A tear trickled down Greta's cheek. "I would love to meet them, as well."

One of Julia's last photographs was a family picture of the five of them in front of Rachel's high school on the day of her graduation. Jackson's features were almost cartoonishly handsome, with his rugged good looks, his thick head of hair, and his crooked grin.

"Is that your husband?" Ella cried with excitement, grabbing the phone.

Julia's throat tightened. "That's Jackson."

"Gosh, he's something. Momma, isn't he something?"

Greta nodded. "I don't care what he looks like, as long as he's a good man."

Julia blinked twice and then forced herself to nod. *What had Jackson done when he'd figured out she wasn't planning on coming home? She imagined him drinking beer in his underwear while Nirvana played on high volume. She imagined him going through their photo albums and guffawing at the stupidity of their previous life.* "I'm off to greener pastures, now..."

"A beautiful family, a publishing house all your own, and probably many creative works up your sleeves," Ella said proudly.

"My girls are really something," Greta affirmed, drawing her hands across both Julia's and Ella's and squeezing tenderly. She then turned her attention back to Julia to add, "It's a good thing you and Charlie broke up when you did. Otherwise, you never would have built this big, beautiful life with Jackson."

It was like a knife stabbed through Julia's stomach. Ella could sense the shift and said quickly, "Oh, but Charlie was such a good guy. The breakup was probably really hard on you."

This subtext was: *We never really knew what happened between you. One day, Charlie returned to Nantucket without you, and we never got to know what happened.*

"I saw Charlie yesterday," Julia said suddenly, surprising all of them.

Greta's lips parted with surprise. "What?"

"He came by the hospital to say hello," she whispered. "I thought it was such a nice gesture."

Greta and Ella exchanged worried glances. Ella sipped her water and set the glass back on the table.

"What's going on?" Julia demanded.

"Honey..." Greta shivered. "Charlie hasn't had as much luck as you have."

"What do you mean?"

"His wife died two years ago," Greta continued. "Poor thing. Such a sweetheart and she left two daughters and Charlie behind. And now, the daughters are off the island. I've heard that Charlie mostly keeps to himself these days, but I suppose I'm one to talk."

Julia's eyes widened with surprise. The server splayed the

charcuterie board between them, exclaiming an eager, "Voila!" and then telling them that she was taking a French class online. Greta and Ella thanked her as Julia continued to stir in her sorrows.

That fateful day at the bus station, Julia and Charlie had embarked on very different journeys.

And neither of those journeys had really turned out the way they'd hoped.

But shouldn't she have learned that as a Copperfield daughter? That life was a meandering journey toward endless disappointment?

"Eat up, Julia..." Greta told her, nudging the platter of cheese. "We're all going to take care of ourselves for a change."

# Chapter Sixteen

That night, Bernard Copperfield refused to leave his upstairs quarters yet again. This was a welcomed relief for Ella, Julia, Danny, Laura, and Greta. They spent the evening chatting, eating a nourishing dinner of clam chowder and fresh bread, and listening to old music that made Greta's cheeks glow with nostalgia. Just before nightfall, the five of them took a little walk along the ocean, their feet sponging in the sands. They caught the eye of several other beach-walkers, who muttered to themselves instinctively. *"I think that was Greta Copperfield. Can you believe it?"*

Greta walked with a pride reminiscent of her previous days as Lady of The Copperfield House. She latched an arm through her grandson Danny's, who guided her evenly over the rougher terrain of the beach before they discovered the safety of the boardwalk.

*This is what Henry should do for his grandmother, Julia thought as she watched them from behind.*

Greta spoke gently to her grandson about his music career

and his belief that if he "didn't make it before the age of twenty-two, then it was all over."

"I don't believe that for a second," Greta told him. "There is no timeline on life."

At this, Ella and Julia exchanged glances, both praying that their mother would heed her own advice. That was always easier said than done.

Just before bed, Ella and Julia met in the hallway between the bedrooms and the bathroom, both with washed and lotion-ed faces that caught the glow of the moonlight.

"Today was nice," Ella began.

"It was really lovely," Julia agreed. "Like something outside of time."

Ella nodded. "The house looks better, as well. Mom was pleased with what we did."

"It's liveable, I guess. Whatever that means in such an old place with so many bad memories," Julia said.

They shared a brief moment of silence, both stewing in their memories, their volatile images of the end of their family's happy era.

"How long do you think you'll stay?" Julia asked Ella then.

Ella shrugged. "Maybe till the end of the week, when I need to get the kids back to the city for school. What about you?"

"I can do almost all my work remotely," Julia told her.

"What about Jackson?"

"He's so busy with his career." Julia tried to make her voice sound calm and casual, as though Jackson's distance from her own life was something she expected and wanted.

Ella's eyes flickered for a moment as though she'd half-guessed the reality of Julia's world.

"Well, let's see how the next few days go," Ella breathed.

"Agreed."

* * *

Several days later, Julia awoke at seven-thirty to an email from her financial advisor, again begging her to "fire all employees and eliminate Orchard Publishing once and for all."

**There's no way out of this mess without a miracle, Julia. Please listen to what I am telling you. I don't want you to fall into financial ruin just because you carried your dream too far into the future.**

**This is a dark patch, Julia, but know this: You will have better times ahead. You know plenty of people in the publishing world who could give you a leg up in their publishing houses. Perhaps you could work as an agent! There's unlimited potential.**

**Give me a call so we can discuss dissolving the business and how best to operate in the following weeks.**

Julia took a deep breath, letting the words sink in, then shut her phone off and stared through the citrus haze of morning light. Greta and Ella's words of excitement for Julia's Midwestern life, her publishing house, her marriage, and her family echoed in Julia's ears. *How could she have allowed everything to crumble? How had she become such a failure?*

Julia wrapped herself in an overlarge sweatshirt, grabbed her laptop, and stepped into the dark shadows of the hallway. For this solitude, Julia was grateful as she tip-toed toward the staircase, rushed downstairs, and brewed herself a big pot of coffee. The bread, cheese, and fruits beckoned her, but her anxiety was so great that eating seemed like a ridiculous concept.

With a black cup of coffee in hand, Julia wandered back

toward the ground floor study, where she and Ella had discovered that pile of manuscripts from the long-ago days of The Copperfield House's artist residency.

This was where she'd begun her career: sitting in front of a big pile of manuscripts, hungry to both dig into the world of literature and help build the future of literature, all at once.

*Could one of these manuscripts be the key to revamping Orchard Publishing?*

*Could one of those writers in their prime in the mid-nineties give her the hope to keep going?*

She laughed to herself. It was such a naive concept. After all, publishing trends had shifted so much in the past twenty-five years. People didn't buy what they used to buy, and therefore, people didn't write what they used to write. All publishers looked for "the next *Hunger Games*" or "the next *Twilight*" and neglected anything with unique promise.

Regardless, Julia began to read the first few pages of the manuscripts from those long-forgotten days. Some of the prose was alarmingly beautiful, if boring— with one woman describing the nature surrounding The Copperfield House with unforeseen poetics. A male writer began a story with the protagonist suffering a heart attack, which had resulted in Bernard Copperfield writing a note beside it: *"We need to feel the pain of this. We need to experience every shocking moment."*

Julia opened her laptop, connected to a hotspot on her phone (as The Copperfield House didn't have WiFi), and searched for some of those ex-Copperfield House writers.

The man who'd written about the heart attack was now a philosophy professor at the University of Virginia.

The woman who'd described the beach with such poetics words was now a manager of an artsy cinema in Austin, Texas.

Other writers had been published a handful of times in the early 2000s before their publishing careers had ceased to exist.

It was a funny thing imagining these writers within the halls of The Copperfield House, all brimming with dreams and creative desires. Eventually, time had had its way with them, and eventually, they'd given up on their dreams.

Julia began to read over the manuscript written by Marcia Conrad, the young woman who'd allegedly had an affair with her father. The writing was snappy and youthful; the story began arrogantly yet had confidence. Had Julia received this manuscript at Orchard Publishing, she might have considered it for publication but would have told the writer it required *"a whole lot of hard edits."*

Before reaching the fifth page, Julia decided to check out where Marcia was in the world. She'd left The Copperfield House with a promise of a job out in Los Angeles, but where had life taken her since then?

Apparently, she'd gone pretty dang far.

That first indie movie she'd worked on had led to a series of films that she was credited with both writing and directing. In the mid-2000s, she wrote and directed her TV show, which had had incredible acclaim. Maybe Julia hadn't heard of it because she'd been deep in the throngs of early motherhood at the time.

Since then, Marcia had written seven novels and directed four more movies. She was slated to co-write a film with Paul Thomas Anderson later that year. And she'd been labeled a *"Woman Entrepreneur Extraordinaire"* by Vogue Magazine the previous year.

Julia's heart surged with emotion.

In the wake of Marcia's time at The Copperfield House, she'd become a prominent artist while so many others had struggled and failed.

*Did she ever think about her friendship with Bernard Copperfield?*

Julia searched for Marcia Conrad's website, which featured

a beautiful black-and-white photograph of the now-fifty-year-old woman. In the photograph, she stood in a romantic alleyway in Paris with her head slung back so that her blonde curls caught the light beaming in through the tops of the Parisian rooftops.

The website listed her accomplishments and awards, her future projects, and various quotes from artists, actors, and directors she'd worked with.

On the final page of the site, a chat box read:

**Reach out to Marcia for a potential project or interview. Remember that Marcia Conrad is first and foremost a feminist and loves to give women a leg-up in the industry.**

Julia arched her brow at the words. *Was Marcia using the concept of feminism as a way to make herself look better? Or did she actually help project women forward in the film and television world?*

With a shrug, Julia began to type out a message to Marcia. What did she have to lose?

*Hi Marcia,*

*You probably don't remember me, but I remember you. You lived in my home on Nantucket Island for ten months back in 1996, where you worked closely with my father, Bernard Copperfield.*

*In the wake of your time at The Copperfield House, I see that you've had a prosperous career. As a woman in publishing, it is marvelous to see other women pushing boundaries the way you have.*

*I hope you don't perceive this message as anything more than me trying to put together the pieces of my family's life. I'm almost forty-three years old now, and I want to move forward to the future while understanding more of the past.*

*What was your relationship with my father? Was he more than just a mentor? Did you have a romantic affair?*

*Any light you could help shed on my father and your time at The Copperfield House would be appreciated.*

*All the best to you,*

*Julia Copperfield*

Julia pressed the send button and leaned back, laughing to herself. There was no way Marcia Conrad would answer that message in a million years. The Copperfield House was no more than a blip in the scope of her successful life.

Down the hall, there came a screech and a cry of excitement. Julia leaped from her chair and hustled for the doorway, where she heard another howl.

"Are you serious?" This was Ella's voice, high-pitched.

Julia stretched her legs toward the foyer as her heart pumped with a mix of fear and joy. When she rounded the corner, she discovered a gorgeous sight.

There, with the front door flung open, stood her two sisters, sharing an embrace.

Alana. Alana Copperfield had come home.

Entranced, Julia walked toward them as they wept with relief. When Ella stepped back, Alana's eyes found Julia's. Julia's knees nearly gave out at the beauty of the woman before her— a woman who'd given her life to the modeling industry before time and age had forced her to quit.

"You're kidding me," Julia breathed before rushing forward to join her sisters' group hug.

Within that embrace, Alana's glorious Parisian perfume nearly made Julia choke. It was such a contrast to the coffee and grime of the previous few days, as though Alana had brought all the magic of Parisian beauty along with her to the sight of a grave.

But when Alana stepped back, adjusting her fashionable hat, her face suddenly scrunched up with emotion. She fell back against the open door, which clunked into the wall behind it.

"Alana? Are you all right?" Ella breathed.

A wail rose out from Alana as her shoulders shook. Ella and Julia exchanged worried glances.

Another Copperfield had returned home after twenty-five years.

And it seemed none of them was handling the abrupt return well.

# Chapter Seventeen

Alana hadn't been able to stop shaking. Julia and Ella planted her on the living room sofa and dressed, donning spring jackets and scarves and pushing their feet into tennis shoes. Alana's feet displayed beautiful heels, the likes of which you couldn't walk on for longer than fifty yards. Julia coaxed Alana into a pair of their mother's tennis shoes, which Alana sneered at before bowing down and tying the laces. A walk was the only thing they could do to clear their heads. A walk would let them know how to proceed.

During the commotion, Greta appeared downstairs, dressed in slacks and a turtleneck and a thick pair of socks. Unlike the previous days since her return from the hospital, she'd applied makeup and styled her hair so that it lost the *"old woman in a haunted house"* vibe and gained a *"regal woman worthy of respect"* vibe. Gripping the end of the staircase railing, she gazed out across the living room at her three beautiful daughters, her eyes wide with shock. One was a musician, another a model, and the last a businesswoman.

"All three of you— here in this house." She shook her head tentatively. "I can hardly believe it."

Alana walked toward her mother in a pair of tennis shoes. She embraced Greta lovingly as tears continued to trail down her cheeks. Greta splayed a hand across her eldest daughter's hair, gobsmacked.

"It's like the curse is over," Greta breathed.

Nobody questioned it. In many ways, the trial had felt like the beginning of a curse.

Minutes later, the four Copperfield women gathered on the beach's edge and blinked out at the frothing waves. Alana was directly to Julia's left, noticeably weeping with every step, yet doing it like an actress in an old movie— as though each tear made her more beautiful than before.

Finally, Alana, always the dramatic one, decided to tell her story.

"I don't know if I can do it anymore."

Julia and Ella exchanged glances. After twenty-five years of no contact, how were they supposed to know what Alana meant?

"Asher was always a dreamer," Alana continued. "When I first met him at The Copperfield House, I had this feeling that we would run off and conquer the world together. And we did. For a time."

"You were such a marvelous model," Greta agreed. "That magazine spread you sent me... I have it somewhere. You exude such magic in that photograph."

Alana sniffled. "Mom, that was over fifteen years ago. I never received much work after that, and the acting dried up soon afterward. And meanwhile, Asher's career, it just skyrocketed."

"That's men for you," Ella breathed.

"I was so happy for a little while," Alana told them. "With his career, we were able to go anywhere, do anything. We moved to Paris but had a flat in New York City, London, and Bejing."

At the mention of Beijing, Julia's ears began to burn.

"He became a prominent artist in every circle," Alana continued. "And with that, his cruelty and manipulation ballooned."

"What?" Ella demanded, aghast.

Alana nodded as her eyes widened. They continued to walk in silence as Alana seemed to stew in what to say next. Before long, they reached the edge of the docks, where lines of sailboats drifted gently in the wind. Greta admitted she needed a moment to sit down, to rest her legs. As she dropped onto a bench, her knees cracked a little.

"Are you okay, Mom?" Julia asked, sitting beside her and placing a hand on her shoulder.

"Of course, darling." Greta grabbed Julia's hand and lifted her gaze to Alana. "Please, Alana. Tell us all you can."

"Let us be there for you," Ella whispered, her voice cracking.

Alana shook her head as the sharp wind off the bay rushed through her hair. She turned back, her eyes glittering with the sight of the water as though she was looking at it for the first time. "I don't know what came over me," she said. "The minute I entered The Copperfield House, it was like I suddenly had to face the truth."

"You must have traveled a long way," Greta offered.

"You have no idea," Alana said mysteriously.

Suddenly, Ella lifted a finger to point out toward the far end of the dock. A handsome man with dark blonde hair stood there, turning a rope around and around his elbow. Julia's heart shattered with recognition.

"Isn't that Charlie Bellows?" Ella asked.

"It sure is," Greta affirmed. "I'd recognize him anywhere."

Alana's eyes shifted toward Julia's. Julia was captivated by him, remembering the strange moments they'd shared at the hospital and the knowledge that he'd lost his wife two years ago. Was it love she now felt for him roaring out from her belly? Or was it devastation at what they'd both lost?

"Are you going to go talk to him?" Alana asked.

Julia shook her head timidly. "No."

"Why not?" Ella asked playfully, trying to lighten the mood. "You said you already saw him the other day, right? I think it's sweet that you two could try to be friends. So much time has passed, after all."

"And besides. Julia's happily married. Aren't you, Julia?"

Alana's words were heavy with sarcasm, so much so that Julia whipped her head around to catch Alana's gaze. Her heart surged with fear.

*Why did she suddenly realize that Alana knew far more about her situation than anyone else?*

Neither Greta nor Ella seemed to sense anything was wrong.

"She is happily married," Ella agreed. "But that doesn't mean she and Charlie didn't have something really beautiful and special. I think it's good to hold onto our memories. It's something I've realized this week, spending so much time with Mom, Julia, and my kids in The Copperfield House."

Julia arched an eyebrow toward Alana, simmering with a mix of anger and confusion. After a long pause, she said, "You um... You said that you have an apartment in Beijing?"

Alana nodded almost imperceptibly. "Asher has an exhibition there right now."

"Right now, huh?"

Alana's eyes glittered strangely.

There was a lurch in Julia's gut.

"I don't suppose you've spent any time in Beijing, have you, Julia?" Alana continued. "Or have any plans to go there any time soon?"

For a moment, Julia thought for sure she would vomit across the sidewalk. Still, neither her mother nor Ella caught the hint.

*Did Alana really travel all the way to Nantucket from Beijing to rub this in her face?*

*Was she really that cruel?*

*Or had she actually come there after something sinister had happened between herself and Asher?*

Julia rose from the bench, her hand across her stomach.

"Julia, sit down," Alana ordered.

"She's going to meet Charlie," Ella said, still in the dark about what had just happened.

"Tell him we say hello," Greta said warmly.

"Julia..." Alana warned.

Julia glanced at her sister before forcing herself down the dock, headed straight for Charlie. Her footfalls made the dock creak beneath her as though the harsh autumn and winter months had damaged the boards too much to allow for human weight.

"Hey! Julia! Let's go get something to eat," Alana called after her, still hovering back by the bench.

As an American woman in Beijing, Alana probably relied on international news to get by. Jackson Crawford was the brand-new face of international news. Her husband, a stranger, delivering international news in that whip-smart and handsome way of his.

It was like something out of a nightmare.

Halfway down the dock, Charlie turned and froze, just as captivated with her as she was with him. But when she was five feet away, she stopped short, too terrified to approach him. It was like there was a forcefield around him, brought on by their trauma from twenty-five years ago.

"I'm sorry I was so weird the other day," Julia apologized suddenly.

In her mind, she thought: *Nothing has worked out, Charlie. Nothing. Can't you see how broken I am?*

Charlie continued to lace the rope around and around his elbow. "I'm sorry I stopped by like that. It was too weird."

"It was weird. But in a good way."

Charlie stopped rolling up the rope again. Julia pressed her hand against her stomach, willing herself not to throw up. She then took in the view of his sailboat, a gorgeous wooden beauty with a high mast that tilted to-and-fro with the breeze off the bay.

"I remember when we used to go out together," she breathed then, transfixed with her memories. "I haven't been out in a boat in years, now. I wonder if I'd even remember how."

Charlie's smile was crooked and playful, endearing in ways Jackson's never was. He paused his tying-up of his rope, arched an eyebrow, and said, "I don't know how much longer you're on the island, but... I could take you out sometime."

The idea of returning to the bench where Alana sat waiting for her sent Julia into spirals. She splayed a hand across her stomach as the dock tilted beneath her.

"Why not right now?"

Julia sat gingerly at the side of the boat and watched as the first man she'd ever loved eased himself through the mechanisms of getting the sailboat out of the harbor. There was the vibrant rush of the wind through the sails, the last creak of the sailboat as it ducked away from the dock, and the water that sloshed against the side of the boat. Although she could feel her sisters' and mother's eyes upon her, she refused to look back, sizzling with exhaustion at the onslaught of memories and Alana's ominous confession that she knew all about Jackson leaving her.

Julia and Charlie fell into an easy silence as they penetrated through the Atlantic waves, heading north from the bay and into the open ocean. Julia watched the supple curve of his muscles and the masculine nature of his hands, which seemed to cover easy territory as he moved from one area of the sailboat to the other, operating the sails. It was hard for Julia to believe that this was the man she'd given everything to back in the day — first kisses, first "I love you's," and everything else that went along with that. Shadowed memories in the back of his old pickup truck flooded through her mind, memories she'd tucked away.

"You're still pretty good at that," she commented after nearly a half-hour of silence, surprising herself.

Charlie laughed gently, turning his eyes toward hers. "I'd hope so. I've been here all this time, you know. Not trapped somewhere on the mainland like other people I know."

"Have you heard of Lake Michigan?" Julia teased back. "There are many boats that sail through that lake."

"And did you ever sail it?"

"No." Julia scrunched her nose as he laughed outright. *Had she lost every ounce of her Nantucket nature?*

Again, they eased back into silence, sailing west along the rush of the waves. Julia had forgotten how poetic sailing could be, that you fell in tune with the salty breeze, spitting waters, and burning bright sun. She tipped her head back, closing her eyes so that she could feel the elements in her very soul.

The facts of her life seemed ridiculous at that moment.

She'd just gotten onto a boat with her ex-boyfriend to retreat from her elder sister.

Both Alana and Ella were back home along with her.

Alana was in an emotionally abusive marriage with a man

she'd met at The Copperfield House more than twenty-five years ago.

And Julia kept her secrets locked tight.

Clouds rumbled over them, splaying out like pie dough and darkening evenly, casting everything in violets and heavy blues. Julia shivered, zipping her coat all the way to her chin. Charlie's eyes widened with surprise.

"I think we might get a bit of—" he began.

But before he finished, the rain began to splatter over them, gluing their coats to their shoulders and back, like second skins and aligning their hair across their foreheads. Julia heard herself scream with a mix of fear and joy as Charlie steadied the sails to keep them from capsizing.

"Julia! Can you grab that—" Charlie began, flailing a hand toward another sail.

Julia rushed for the rope and tugged it, making the sail much smaller based on what she'd thought were long-forgotten instincts. Her stomach ballooned with fear as she was cast to her knees suddenly, smashing herself against the wooden boards. It all happened so fast.

Charlie appeared over her in a flash, helping her to her feet. His strong, capable hands lifted her and placed her gently on the side of the boat. "Hold onto this pole," he instructed her, sensing how dazed she was.

She felt like a child, tossed around on the water and growing all the more distant from any sense of responsibility.

And with this distance to herself and to her rational mind, she found herself saying things she might never have said.

"Charlie..." she breathed. "Charlie, I'm just... I'm just so..."

Charlie dropped down and placed his hands on her elbows, probably as a way to steady her.

"I'm so sorry for what happened to you," she told him simply.

Charlie's eyes glittered with understanding. This was about his wife's death.

Charlie then shook his head and spoke just loud enough for Julia to hear over the screaming winds.

"I'm so sorry I left you, Julia. All those years ago, I left you alone in Manhattan."

Julia shook her head, struck by the emotion that welled through her. "Your mother..." she began before stopping altogether. She couldn't get the words out, the words that forgave him for what he'd done. The words that showed just how much she understood, especially now, why he'd left.

Their eyes shone with emotion as their clothing sopped against them. With their noses mere inches from one another, Julia thought they might kiss. But instead, Charlie traced a wet strand of hair around her ear lovingly, the way he'd done all those years ago. It was like he'd been waiting to do that all along, as a way to reach into the past and unite them again.

*But there was never going back, was there?* That was certainly the theme of the week.

"Let's try to sail back without capsizing." Charlie stood to his feet to operate the sails and steer them back to shore. "You never know what the winds will bring. Especially this far out to sea."

# Chapter Eighteen

To Julia's surprise, her mother, Alana, and Ella awaited her at the docks in Ella's idling station wagon. Ella waved a hand through the flailing rain and flashed her lights as Julia and Charlie hustled off the docks, both slippery as fishes. When they reached the edge of the parking area, Charlie ruffled a hand through his dark blonde hair and said, "Well. It was good to do that once, for old time's sake." The words sucked the air out of Julia's lungs. He then gave a timid wave to the rest of the Copperfield clan and turned back toward wherever his vehicle was parked, disappearing through the gray fog of the rain.

Julia's heart cracked all over again at the sight of him disappearing.

She hadn't been allowed to explain herself.

It had been just another awkward encounter.

"Julia! Come on!" Ella called through the window.

Julia dove into the back of the station wagon, apologizing profusely about her drenched state. Greta sat in the back with a bunch of soft towels and began to help Julia clean up, draping one over her shoulders and dotting the back of her neck. It was so mothering, this moment, that Julia closed her eyes and allowed her head to drape back.

"What the heck was that?" Ella finally asked with a laugh.

"Our adventurous Julia went on a wild ride," Alana teased.

Julia arched an eyebrow toward Alana, disgruntled slightly but no longer angry about what Alana had seen in Beijing. Alana was more-or-less a stranger, and parts of Julia were coming to terms with Jackson's departure. Every day felt like a jagged edge.

When they returned to The Copperfield House, they discovered Danny and Laura in the living room, sitting pin-straight and staring ahead blankly, as though they'd just seen a ghost. Laura lifted a finger toward the doorway between the living room and the greater kitchen area, just as the sound of a knife slashed through something thick.

Even the speaker system was on, playing an old album from Electric Light Orchestra. Julia would have known the song anywhere, as it always took her back to long-lost days at The Copperfield House. Especially the days when her father decided to cook.

"He's downstairs?" Ella breathed toward her children, shocked.

"He hardly looked at us," Danny informed them. "Just came down the back staircase and started working on dinner."

Greta walked timidly to the center of the living room and lifted her chin, listening to the sounds of the man she'd once loved as he worked through the schedule of dinner— the chop of the vegetables, the first sizzle of a skillet.

One of Greta and Bernard's love languages had been cooking for one another. Everyone knew that.

"Any idea what he's making?" Alana asked Danny.

"I peeked in a few minutes ago. It looks like duck," Laura answered for him.

"Gosh. I have a feeling he's making Duck à l'Orange." Greta breathed.

Overwhelmed with courage from her strange sailboat adventure with Charlie, Julia stepped down the hallway and appeared in the kitchen doorway, where a swarm of delicious dinner smells came over her. Sure enough, Bernard Copperfield himself was in the throes of cooking, slicing and dicing vegetables and large, vibrant oranges. Two six-pound ducks sat, trimmed of excess fat as the oven pre-heated below.

He was making Greta's favorite, a recipe she'd mastered during their time together in Paris.

According to family lore, Bernard had never managed to make it as well as Greta, although he'd tried time and time again. "It's why I need to keep her around," he'd said back in the old days. "I'm still studying her Duck à l'Orange."

"Dad..." Julia murmured from the doorway.

Bernard turned slowly, his eyes curious and faraway.

"Do you need any help with this?"

Bernard shook his head and then turned his knife toward the dining room.

"We could set the table?" Julia asked timidly.

"Yes. That would be a great help." Bernard then returned to his slicing and dicing, clearly out of practice with small talk and unwilling to try.

*What was there to talk about in prison? What kinds of conversations had the "great novelist" Bernard Copperfield had over the past twenty-five years?*

It was like he was a shadow of his previous self.

Wordless, Julia headed upstairs to don dry clothes, then returned downstairs to set the table. Ella followed her lead, giving her curious looks as they placed the china around the antique table. Alana stood in the living room corner with her arms crossed severely over her chest.

"What was all that stuff about Beijing?" Ella hissed over the dining room table. "Back on the docks?"

Julia shook her head. "I don't know. But I never really understood Alana."

* * *

There was a sense of doom over the household, as though this dinner with Bernard was a punishment they all had to go through together. Poor Laura and Danny sat side-by-side at the dinner table, texting furiously under the table, probably to one another. Alana had reapplied the makeup she'd cried off and sat model-like and coldly next to Greta, who looked on the verge of a breakdown herself. Julia and Ella sat side-by-side in the same chairs they'd always chosen for themselves back in the old days of The Copperfield House.

And all the while, Bernard bustled in and out, positioning the duck and the roasted Brussels sprouts and the white rice pilaf and the fresh bread across the table. He then uncorked a bottle of Bordeaux, an old favorite of Greta's, and poured a tiny bit into her glass to allow her to try it first.

It seemed like a sweet gesture. Perhaps if anyone else had performed it, it would have been.

But this was Bernard Copperfield.

And no amount of sweet gestures could make the rest of the Copperfield family forget.

Greta lifted the glass of wine and dropped her head back to sip. With her eyes closed, her face twisted up against the sharp memory of the flavor. Julia had read once that taste and smell were inextricably linked to the memory sectors of the brain.

There was no telling where this taste of wine had taken Greta back to.

But when her eyes opened into slits, it was clear that the memories were painful ones.

Bernard waited hesitantly, his large hands wrapped around the bottle. Slowly, Greta returned her glass of wine to the table as silence swelled around them. The only sound was the click-click of Laura and Danny texting one another under the table.

"You made Duck à l'Orange," Greta breathed suddenly, speaking mostly to the gorgeous dinner display rather than to her husband.

Bernard didn't speak. He looked half-petrified.

Nearly a minute passed before Greta spoke again. Throughout that time, hardly anyone at the table dared to breathe.

Greta finally lifted her chin toward her husband, her eyes still in slits as she hissed, "How could you?"

It was like she'd sucked all the air out of Bernard's lungs. His shoulders dropped forward; his cheeks sunk in. He placed the bottle of wine back on the table as Greta continued to speak.

"You think you can just come back into my life after all this time and make... Duck à l'Orange? Really, Bernard. You've been hiding away upstairs for over a week like some sort of ghost. And now you come downstairs to make my favorite meal from all those years ago... As though we could pick up right where we left off?"

Julia and Ella locked eyes for a moment. This was going even worse than she'd imagined, and Ella seemed to think the same.

"You ruined my life, Bernard!" Greta continued, flailing her napkin back so that it fell across the floor. "You ruined my life and our children's lives. Our family split up for twenty-five years because of you. And now you think you can just come back and make... Duck à l'Orange? Like nothing happened? Like we've been enjoying all this family time together since 1996?"

Each time she said Duck à l'Orange, it sounded like an

insult. Now, she jumped up from her chair, pushing it so much that it fell to the floor behind her, then marched out of the dining room angrily, leaving the rest of them in the awkward shell of silence.

Bernard moved slowly toward the window and wrapped his hands behind his back. He breathed after a long and somber moment, "If only I could explain..."

"Explain what, Dad?" Alana asked, exasperated.

There was no empathy in her tone.

Heavy with failure, Bernard retreated to the back staircase and headed back to his quarters alone. The smell of his cologne remained in the room as the duck cooled across its platter, stunning and cooked to perfection.

After another long and strained moment, Ella whispered, "I think it would be a waste of a meal if we don't eat it."

"What if he poisoned it?" Alana pointed out.

"He was trying to build a bridge..." Julia said. "Between himself and the rest of us."

"Well, he isn't a very good architect," Alana offered.

Ella rolled her eyes at Alana's comment as she stood to begin serving the duck. "I don't know that Mom will ever forgive him."

"I don't know how she could," Alana said.

"I think it's up to us to help them create a plan," Julia said simply, her heart-shattering. "They can't stay in this house together without speaking. It would drive anyone insane."

"Any ideas of what to do?" Ella asked.

Julia shook her head as Ella splayed a slab of meat across her plate. Across from her, Laura slid a knife through the tender duck and took a small bite, and the shock of the flavor made her face grow slack.

"Wow..." she breathed. "Did he take a cooking class in prison or something?"

There was a moment of silence as the rest of them dug into

the duck, which had been cooked to perfection. Memories of so long ago at The Copperfield House came over the three Copperfield daughters, who hardly looked up at one another. Maybe the images of the past were too heavy.

Midway through the meal, Julia's phone buzzed with an email. As she chewed a tender morsel of duck, she opened it to read:

**Julia Copperfield,**

**My name is Florian Goldstatt, and I am the legal representative for Marcia Conrad.**

**We've received your inquiry regarding the past personal matters of Marcia Conrad and would like to advise you to cease all contact with Ms. Conrad immediately.**

**If you proceed with your contact, there will be legal consequences.**

**Sincerely,**

**Florian Goldstatt**

Julia's jaw dropped wide open with surprise.

"Julia? What is it?" Ella asked.

Julia shoved her phone into her pocket, then made up some story about Rachel's decision to drop her French minor. "She loves speaking French." Julia heard herself say.

But in truth, her head raced with intrigue. Why would a successful filmmaker and screenwriter go out of her way to have her lawyer send Julia a cease contact letter? She'd only asked a question about her long-ago relationship with Bernard Copperfield, so it didn't make any sense. This was especially strange because she'd expected Marcia to either read the email and not respond or ignore it altogether.

Why would she take such dramatic action against a silly email? It didn't add up.

# Chapter Nineteen

harlie returned to the house on Lincoln soaked to the bones. He peeled himself off his truck's front seat and hustled through the rain to the front door, which remained unlocked. Once inside the foyer, he slammed the door closed as waves of frustration billowed through him.

*What the heck was that?*

Julia... He and Julia Copperfield had carved out space for one another again, their noses so close they nearly touched and the energy between them alive and pulsing with life and promise. *"I'm so sorry for everything that's happened to you,"* she'd said, insinuating that she knew all about the pain he'd endured over the last two years or so. Shame and sorrow flowed through him. *What a fool she probably thought he was.*

"Dad?"

Charlie froze at the sound. For the first time, he focused on the matter at hand: the warm swell of roasting vegetables in the kitchen, the soft twinkling of the speaker system playing a pop song, and the joyous laughter of his twenty-year-old twin daughters, Zoey and Willa, who had come home to surprise him.

His blonde-haired daughters appeared in the doorway between the foyer and the kitchen to discover their father a sopping mess. Zoey giggled as Willa walked to the hallway to collect a handful of towels.

"Did you fall in the ocean, Daddy?" Zoey asked.

Charlie accepted the towels from Willa as a grin crept up his cheeks. "I didn't know I would have surprise visitors today."

"We can tell you weren't expecting us or anyone else, for that matter," Willa chimed in. "You're out of almost everything, food-wise. No coffee, either. We made a run to the grocery store for essentials." Willa collected a lock of hair behind her ear and blinked expectantly at him as though she'd assumed him to be much more responsible than he was. "How were you planning to keep yourself alive after today?"

Charlie laughed outright. After a moment's awkward pause, he finally said, "My girls are home!" in a voice that made both girls leap toward him, throwing their arms around him joyously, no longer frightened of how wet he was or how lonely he seemed.

Charlie took a hot shower, dressed in pajama pants and a t-shirt, and returned to the kitchen to find his girls serving out a platter of roasted vegetables, feta, hummus, and fresh bread. Willa suggested that he hadn't had any nutrients in some time before adding that Zoey had avoided vegetables for the better part of the winter.

"I'm trying to force-feed her nutrients, Daddy," Willa told him as they sat around the kitchen table. "But she won't eat anything but Pop-Tarts."

"I think I understand why," Charlie began.

Willa's jaw dropped. "Don't you dare give her an easy out."

"What can she do? Pop-Tarts are delicious," Charlie said with a laugh.

"You two are impossible," Willa moaned as she slathered hummus along the edge of her plate.

Charlie allowed himself to fall into the warm cocoon of his daughters' voices, squabbling over the same silly arguments they'd had for years, talking about the classes they were taking that semester, and dreaming up ways to redecorate the apartment they shared. In some ways, they spoke like their mother, with a similar rhythm and a similar song. In other ways, they were uniquely themselves, his pride and joy, his everything.

"Looks like the rain's clearing up," Willa noted as she lifted her eyes to the kitchen window.

"The soil will be perfect for the flowers in a couple of hours," Zoey offered.

"That's what I was thinking," Willa returned.

"What flowers?" Charlie asked.

Zoey and Willa shot their father a strange glance. Charlie's heart quickened. Had he said something wrong?

"We want to plant new flowers at Mom's grave," Willa answered.

"You know how much Mom loved spring flowers," Zoey told him.

Charlie watched timidly as his daughters gathered the used plates and the now-empty platter and headed off to the kitchen sink to wash them. Charlie hadn't bothered to cook anything in a few months, and it was strange to see the kitchen in such use. Bubbles floated from the kitchen sink toward the front window, popping against the glass.

Charlie carried the weight of his sorrow for his wife's death across his shoulders and within his stomach. Hours later, he stood hunched forward at the flower shop, watching as his daughter's selected tulips to plant at their mother's grave, arguing briefly about which colors worked best. Charlie wondered why they seemed to carry the death so easily, knowing what to do and how best to decorate without even a single tear. His conclusion was that they'd both been able to build lives elsewhere, off the island. This had saved them while he'd wallowed in the painful reality of loneliness.

Willa placed a big plastic sheet down in front of their mother's grave, where they positioned their knees and tore through the mud, removing last year's flowers and replacing them with a fresh batch of tulips. Zoey and Willa worked dutifully, chatting amicably about their mother and what she'd taught them about gardening over the years. Charlie did what he could until he eventually sat back, recognizing that this was something the girls wanted to do themselves. They didn't need him.

The grave he'd selected for Sally was a simple one with the slightest of details at the top, plus an engraving at the bottom that read: *"A mother's love never ends."*

"We should say something to her," Willa told them, leaning back, rubbing her hands across a towel to remove the gunk and soil.

"I'll go first," Zoey said. "Mom. I wish you were here so you could help me talk Willa into not going on any more dates with Jeffrey Ballard. He's literally an accountant major. I mean, how much more boring can you get?"

Willa groaned and added, "Mom, I wish you were here so you could help me talk some sense into Zoey and tell her that actually, I want to date someone with a stable career because I want children and a house one day."

"Mom..." Zoey laughed outright as the girls' eyes met.

Charlie's heart was squeezed with sorrow. He turned his eyes toward the tulips, which glowed with the fresh new light of the April afternoon. It was hope after a rain storm. *Why, then, did he feel such darkness?*

His wife should have been there for these conversations with her twenty-one-year-old daughters.

His wife should have lived to be one hundred years old.

Charlie shivered as his daughters continued to speak to the

grave, telling Sally how much they missed her and their plans for their summers and their hopes for their futures.

After a time, Willa nudged Charlie and asked what he wanted to say. Charlie's tongue became dry. His heart ached, heavy with emotions of love and longing and fear. Only a few hours ago, he and Julia had stood out in a sudden and violent storm as the winds thrust the boat across the waves. Now, he sat before Sally's grave and tried to believe in something, anything beyond his fear that his life was now over.

"I love you, Sally," he whispered. "And I will miss you every day of my life."

After they'd washed their hands of soil back at the house on Lincoln, Willa and Zoey sat Charlie down at the kitchen table with a mug of hot cocoa and asked him if he was really okay.

"I'm just fine," he told them simply.

Willa and Zoey exchanged glances. Willa then continued, "We've heard some rumors that you've been... how should we put this?"

"Kind of a hermit," Zoey finished.

"Not meeting your friends anymore," Willa added.

"Keeping to yourself."

Charlie's stomach twisted. It was one thing to feel the depths of sorrow and loneliness; it was a whole other thing to have your twenty-year-old daughters accost you for it. In a word, he felt tragic.

"You girls know that I'm addicted to my work," he finally told them.

"You work nine to five most days," Willa pointed out. "What do you do the rest of the time?"

Charlie shrugged. He tried to add up all the hours of the days of his life but came up blank. He couldn't very well tell his daughters, *"It kind of depends on the specials at the diner and what's on TV."* It was too pathetic.

"We just love you so much, Dad," Zoey confessed, her eyes marred with concern.

"Mom dying was so awful," Willa added. "But both Zoey and I have been going to on-campus therapy to try to deal with it."

"Sometimes, it doesn't feel like it helps at all," Zoey said. "But other times, I can feel myself making headway and finding peace within myself. If that makes sense."

"I don't know about therapy." Charlie began.

"We know you're old-fashioned," Willa piped up. "But if you could just start with little things, to push yourself forward. Join a club or meet a friend for a beer or..."

"Anything," Zoey affirmed.

"There's still so much to live for," Willa told him.

Charlie's tongue dried out all over again. He exhaled all the air from his lungs as images of Julia out on his sailboat flashed through his memory.

"I just don't know if I have it in me," Charlie told them simply.

"All we're asking is for you to try, Dad," Zoey pleaded.

# Chapter Twenty

Sunday morning, Julia sat on a bench at the ferry docks and watched Ella give her children final hugs goodbye. From this distance, the image of the three of them was striking, with Laura's hair glistening in the morning light and Danny stoic and tall beside her— headed toward manhood, full-speed ahead.

"She looks so cool in that leather jacket, doesn't she?" Alana was seated beside Julia, sipping a cappuccino. "Like she never really had to grow up. I wish she'd tell me her secret."

Julia toyed with the outer edge of her black peacoat, which now seemed middle-aged and Midwestern, all at once. She'd once thought it looked chic.

"Alana..." Julia began tentatively, forcing herself to ask more about what Alana had seen in Beijing.

Alana turned her eyes toward Julia's with curiosity. When the silence grew deafening, Alana replied without emotion, "I won't tell them. It's your news to share. And believe me when I tell you. You're not the only Copperfield child with a life that didn't turn out the way you planned."

Before Julia could respond, Ella joined them, dropping down on the bench beside Julia and waving a hand toward the ferry. "I know I look like an idiot. Why would my seventeen-year-old and eighteen-year-old come out on deck and wave to me?"

But just as she finished, both Danny and Laura appeared on the top deck and waved their palms to and fro as their smiles spread across their faces. Ella stood up from the bench to flail her arm, even more, making both Laura and Danny cackle so loudly that you could hear it over the water.

"They're good kids," Julia complimented as the boat eased out of sight, back northwest toward the mainland.

"They're just happy I let them take the car back to the city," Ella joked. "Who knows what type of mischief they'll get into on the way there?"

"They're seventeen and eighteen years old," Julia offered with a sigh.

"As old as you were when you went to the city alone," Alana said thoughtfully. "And about as old as I was when Asher took me away."

Ella, Alana, and Julia held the silence. Another ferry boat pulled into the docks, and workers hustled out, latching the rope to the wooden slats. They worked tirelessly like a colony of ants, each knowing their purpose without doubting a thing.

"I've been thinking we should call Quentin," Alana announced, breaking their reverie.

Julia and Ella gaped at her.

"Are you insane?" Ella demanded.

Alana shrugged. "Mom and Dad are going off the rails, and I'm a wreck after leaving Asher behind in Beijing. Do you think we could really patch this up ourselves?"

Ella and Julia exchanged glances. *How was it that Alana could insult them both and reason with them at the same time?*

It was a quality her older sister had, and she couldn't understand it.

"When was the last time either of you talked to Quentin?" Julia asked.

"Will and I tried to meet Quentin and his wife for dinner a few years ago. He lives just across the bridge in Manhattan. It seemed ridiculous not to just try to forge some kind of friendship," Ella murmured.

"How did that go?" Julia asked.

Ella scoffed. "Well, let's put it this way. Halfway through appetizers, someone Quentin wanted to impress in the news world walked into the restaurant. Quentin immediately demanded that they join tables with us and spent the rest of the time associating with him. Will and I had no idea what to do. I don't think Quentin's wife knew what to do, either. She seemed embarrassed."

"Poor woman," Julia breathed.

"I still think we should contact him," Alana told them. "We're all here together, trying to clean up the mess. Quentin doesn't get a pass, just because he'd already been gone a few years when it all happened."

"He ran back to LA and never looked back," Julia murmured.

"He helped Mom out with some bills for a while," Alana reported.

"What!" Ella cried. "I didn't know that."

"I think it was survivor's guilt," Alana quipped.

"We all survived it," Julia tried. "It's just that we're all damaged because of it."

"Emotionally crippled is how my therapist put it," Ella added.

Alana flipped her hair behind her shoulders. "Everyone has problems."

They shared this silence for a moment. The ferry in front

of them had filled up with brand-new passengers, ready to set off for the mainland. Julia remembered the trapped feeling she'd once had while growing up on the island. And really, what was stopping her now from running headlong toward that ferry, leaping on, and never returning?

She just had nothing to run toward anymore.

"Let's just think about it for a little while," Julia suggested.

"Okay. Let's go back to the house, then." Alana stood, positioning her Chanel bag across her shoulder before tapping her heels out toward Julia's parked SUV.

"She's probably right, isn't she?" Ella finally asked.

"I just feel like there has to be another way," Julia murmured.

"Do you have any suggestions? I mean, the facts are all right there. Dad's extended an olive branch; Mom's refused it for a good reason. She spent a night in the hospital due to all this stress. Dad's becoming a textbook hermit, and he probably needs years of therapy to get over twenty-five years of prison. I can't bring Mom to New York with me. Alana seems to be in the middle of marital turmoil herself. And you..."

Julia arched her brow, waiting for Ella to deliver a blow about her reality.

But in truth, Ella didn't know anything, did she?

"Well, you're so busy with your publishing house and your husband. You only just became an empty-nester."

"And it's not like Mom wants to live in Bartlett, Illinois," Julia pointed out, relieved that Ella knew nothing about her situation.

"I hate to say it, but you're right. She's an east coaster," Ella affirmed. "Like you used to be."

"Girls? I'm starving!" Alana called from the SUV.

"The queen calls," Ella teased as she searched through her pockets for her car keys.

* * *

When they arrived back at The Copperfield House, they discovered that their mother had laid down for a nap, and their father had again latched himself away in his upstairs study. This left the three sisters to slice and dice vegetables for a stir fry, which they ate in front of the television in the living room, watching a movie they'd all loved as teenagers: *Pretty in Pink.*

"It's such a shame she goes with James Spader at the end," Ella commented.

"I know. The way Duckie looks at her breaks my heart," Julia agreed.

"Are you kidding me? James Spader is so handsome. She would have been a fool not to go with James," Alana told them. "He's still got it now, too. Have you seen him in *The Blacklist*? Bald, yes. Beautiful? Yes."

Ella and Julia giggled, their bellies seizing up. Alana, who'd realized how silly she sounded, howled with laughter as well. For a moment, it was difficult to tell what year it was in The Copperfield House, with all three Copperfield daughter's silly laughter. It might have been 1995 all over again. How Julia wished they could go back in time.

Suddenly, Greta appeared on the landing of the circular staircase in a light pink robe, rubbing her eyes.

"Is that the sound of my girls' laughing?"

"Come down here, Mama," Ella called gently. "We're finishing up *Pretty in Pink.*"

"Gosh. I haven't seen that movie in years," Greta murmured as she continued toward the couch. She dropped down and leaned her head gently against Ella's shoulder as Ella ruffled her gray hair.

Julia's heart seized with longing.

This was another glimpse into the past. This was the heart

and soul of the Copperfield family. This was the love they should have had for the past two and a half decades.

Greta reached for the remote when the movie finished and said, "I think there's a special on this afternoon." She flicked through the stations as Julia stretched to reach her toes.

"What kind of special?" Ella asked, feigning enthusiasm. It was a rare thing to see their mother excited about anything.

"You'll see..." Greta continued to flick through the stations as her eyes caught the reflection of the television.

"Ah. Here it is." Greta stopped at a public news station, which now showed a commercial for Cheez-Its.

"Oh. Now I'm hungry," Alana whispered.

"Shh," Greta hissed as the television flicked onto its main broadcast.

It was an empty stage under a blue light. On the stage, a desk sat with a single chair behind it. Julia's heart seized with terror.

She knew, suddenly, what they were about to see.

The handsome Quentin Copperfield, a man beloved nationwide for his morning talk show, stepped out onto the stage. The flash of his smile aligned with the buttoning of his suit jacket in the front, an action he'd probably performed in front of the mirror countless times. Julia remembered when he'd been a teenager, watching himself in the hall mirror as he'd sauntered toward the steps.

"There he is. My handsome son!" Greta whispered, enraptured.

"Good afternoon, America," Quentin began, his voice sturdy, one you just had to trust. "Welcome to The Sunday Lives, a bi-monthly news show with a different anchor each and every time. It is my honor to be your host. My name is Quentin Copperfield. Many of you probably know me from your morning breakfast rituals, morning commutes, or mornings after a long night on the third shift. Regardless, here on

The Sunday Lives, we have something very different planned for you than your typical daily updates and weather forecasts. Today, I will interview someone incredibly special, someone who has emulated an honorable life here in America. This person is not an actress, athlete, or even a medical doctor. This person is a teacher."

"Oh, come on," Ella muttered to herself.

"Shhh," Greta hissed again.

A woman in her mid-fifties, wearing a black skirt, a black turtleneck, and a green vest with little plaques on the back, walked onto the stage as the audience roared.

"What do you have there on your back, Mrs. Randall?" Quentin asked.

Mrs. Randall turned around to show the plaques. Each were unique, spelling out the name of each of the children in her fifth-grade class.

"That's so sweet, isn't it?" Greta breathed.

Quentin welcomed the woman with a series of initial questions— why she'd wanted to become a teacher, the state of the teaching industry in the United States, and what she adored most about her career. Throughout the interview, Quentin was articulate and smooth, showing his empathy for the situation of many teachers across the continent and his outrage at the limitations of the salary.

"It's easy for him to feel like that," Ella breathed into Julia's ear. "He makes more than any of us combined. He could pay for the entire fifth-grade class college tuitions."

Julia had to admit that Quentin was a smooth talker and damn good at his job. For years, when Jackson had been nothing but an up-and-coming journalist in Chicago, he'd begged her to introduce him to Quentin Crawford. Julia had refused. Thank goodness.

Toward the end of the interview, Mrs. Randall looked directly into the camera to say, "We need the next generation to get excited about teaching again. We need you to recognize the beauty in passing along knowledge and building a better future. We've never been anything without our teachers, and we'll never go anywhere without them."

"I think I speak for everyone when I say that we salute you for your efforts every day," Quentin told her before turning his face toward the camera to announce a commercial break. "Stay tuned after these messages, ladies and gentlemen. We've only just begun The Sunday Lives."

"Shoot," Alana breathed. "He's actually pretty good."

"He's the greatest," Greta affirmed. "When I woke up in time for it, I used to watch him every morning."

Julia closed her eyes at the painful thought of a mother watching her son on the television every day, not able to see him in person.

There was no way around it. They had to find a way to drag Quentin back home.

Later that night, the three Copperfield daughters gathered around the table and positioned a phone face-up in front of Alana. They'd decided that Alana would be the face of the call, as she and Quentin had always been closer due to their ages. Plus, Quentin thought Alana was off in Paris somewhere, living the life of her dreams. He respected her for that.

To their surprise, Quentin answered on the second ring.

"Alana! It's so good to hear your voice. Isn't it sometime past midnight over there?"

It was like the man from the television had crawled into Alana's cell phone. Julia shivered, clutching her elbows.

"Hi, Quentin." Alana put on her model-actress voice, which was bound to work with Quentin. "How have you been?"

They exchanged pleasantries for a few minutes. Quentin bragged about his success while Ella rolled her eyes and opened and closed her mouth, mimicking him.

"Are you ever going to tell him?" Ella hissed, barely enough for anyone to hear.

Quentin, being Quentin, sensed the shift.

"Is someone else there, Alana? Am I on speaker?"

Alana stuttered, her eyes widening. "Listen, Quentin. This isn't an ambush, but I have Ella and Julia here. We're— we're at the house."

On the other end, Quentin held the silence. Julia half-expected him to hang up the phone.

"Hi, Ella. Hi, Julia." Quentin sounded dumbfounded. "You're at... The Copperfield House?"

Alana sighed and explained what she could.

That their mother was mentally, physically, and emotionally ill. That their father refused to leave his study. They needed to figure out what to do next, and they couldn't leave their parents together in this state. On top of it all, the house looked like it could fall apart at any given moment.

"We need you here, Quentin." Alana finally said, her voice pleading. "We need to get the family back together again. Just one last time."

# Chapter Twenty-One

Quentin agreed to come to Nantucket Island to help deal with the Mom and Dad situation. He would leave that Wednesday after his early-morning appearance on the New York City morning show. This left Julia, Ella, and Alana jittery and nervous over the next few days, throwing themselves into revamping the house the best they knew how. They did some deep cleaning, throwing out broken pieces of furniture and having a plumber over to fix a leaky sink in the back bathroom. When the plumber entered, his eyes widened to take stock of the old house, which hardly anyone had entered in twenty-five years. Just his luck, though: the entire place sparkled with cleanliness, its antiques stood shiny and clean, and the paintings hung straight on the walls. His disappointment at how normal everything looked was palpable. Probably, he'd taken the job just to leech up gossip, which he'd planned to pass along to the residents of Nantucket as a form of currency.

Although they still hadn't seen much of their father, they sensed his presence in small ways. Between Monday evening and Tuesday morning, someone had eaten an entire bag of cashews, which just happened to be Bernard Copperfield's favorite snack. Wine bottles were constantly disappearing, as with the olives from the refrigerator. Julia found herself at the grocery store, stocking up on items her father might like. She wished she could have asked him what it felt like, tasting an olive for the first time in twenty-five years. It was probably like a religious experience.

Tuesday night before Quentin's arrival, Nantucket enjoyed its first seventy-degree day since spring had begun. Julia opened up the back patio, which offered a gorgeous view of the beach and the ocean, its waves frothing up across the sands, and set to work cleaning off the patio furniture. She fluttered a beautiful patterned cloth over the back table and set a bouquet of flowers in the center. Admiring her work, she poured herself a glass of rosé, crossed her legs, and sat at the table alone as the breeze fluttered over the tips of her ears.

That's when she heard it.

From somewhere skyward came the sound of classical music.

Julia strained her ears to hear it through the rush of the waves and the sweep of the breeze.

The twinkling music eased itself into grandiose chords and swells. Julia's heart shattered at the sounds of it, recognizing it at last as Rachmaninoff, her father's favorite composer.

Julia stepped outside and walked through the grassy sands to stand beneath her father's open window. The music streamed out of the window, joining with the soft light of the April evening in a way that felt heavenly and dreamlike. Julia pressed her hand across her heart, remembering exactly what her father had said about Rachmaninoff back in her youth.

*"He turns your heart inside out and then hands it back to you."*

Julia had avoided Rachmaninoff for years, as the tremendous agony of some of the music took her straight back to those long-lost days at The Copperfield House. It took her back to her love for her father.

Yet here it all was again, crashing back into her.

Julia went back inside and found herself hovering over a blank sheet of paper, a pen lifted.

Finally, she forced herself to write a note that she eventually slipped beneath his door.

*The past twenty-five years have stolen my heart, turned it inside out, wrung it, and smashed it against the rocks.*

*I've only just gotten my heart back.*

*I hope one day we'll find the strength to talk again.*

*Julia*

\* \* \*

It wasn't outrageous to learn that Quentin Copperfield had flown out to Nantucket from New York City. The likes of Quentin Copperfield wouldn't have been caught in a car that long— and he certainly wouldn't have driven himself. He was just that important.

He arrived at one p.m. sharp in a pair of khakis and a polo shirt, his hair perfectly styled and his cologne something Alana called, "Out of this world expensive."

He stood in front of The Copperfield House with his large hands on his hips. The three sisters eyed him suspiciously as though he was a wolf about to attack.

True to her goodness, Greta was the first to interrupt the awkwardness. She burst from the front door and rushed for her son, her firstborn. He'd been the reason she and Bernard had left Paris in the first place. A surprise pregnancy and a new life on Nantucket, where Greta had been born and raised.

Greta's tears flowed freely yet quietly. With the final

Copperfield there at her doorstep, there was no denying the truth. They were all basically strangers.

One after another, Alana, Julia, and Ella stepped up to give Quentin side hugs. Julia nearly choked on the toxicity of his cologne. Hugging him felt like hugging a slab of marble as he'd sculpted each muscle to perfection in the gym.

"It doesn't look half-bad around here," Quentin noted as he stepped into the house's foyer, leading the way. His ego seemed to swell around the rest of them, forcing them to keep their distance.

"The girls have given me a hand fixing everything up," Greta said, her voice losing traction. "I'll admit, I let some things go around here over the years."

Julia and Ella had prepared lunch for Quentin's arrival, a vibrant salad with arugula, feta, olives, cherry tomatoes, and sandwiches made of turkey and cheese. Throughout the lunch preparation, Alana had sat at the kitchen table in a satin robe and texted aggressively with a French friend who'd reportedly seen Asher around Paris. "I'm sure it's fine. Everyone needs space. We've taken space from our marriage before," Alana had explained to her sisters. Ella and Julia had exchanged worried glances. Alana's mental state seemed precarious but couldn't be their main focus at the moment.

Out at the back patio table, Quentin announced he wasn't eating bread at the moment but would "nibble" on some salad. Greta teetered toward the table as her color shifted. Julia helped her sit in the chair beside Quentin and placed two sandwiches on her plate.

"You've got to eat something, Mom. You're as pale as a ghost," Julia told her.

Greta nodded, took a tentative bite, then placed the sandwich back down. With all four of her children's eyes upon her, she shivered anxiously and brushed a strand of hair behind her ear.

"It's so good to see you four together again..." she whispered. "It's enough to make a mother wonder..." She shook her head despairingly and glanced back toward the door.

"Do you want to lay down for a while, Mom?" Ella asked, erupting from her chair quickly so that it creaked against the floor. "We can bring your sandwiches inside."

Greta splayed a hand across Quentin's. The contrast of her pale, almost greenish skin against his robust, tan hand was alarming.

"We can catch up later, Mom," Quentin told her. "Why don't you let Ella take you to bed?"

Greta looked like a child who'd gotten sick on her birthday. Slowly, she stood, linked her arm through Ella's, and headed for the soft gray embrace of the indoors. For a long moment, the silence grew denser and more toxic over the back patio table. Julia couldn't bring herself to look at Quentin. She could tell he was fuming.

"This is ridiculous," he finally said, his voice powerful, as though he spoke to the entire nation instead of just Alana and Julia.

"She's just shocked to see you. She's been doing a lot better. Don't base judgment on the first ten minutes." Julia told him.

But it was no use. Quentin puffed out his cheeks, exasperated. "I've come today to tell you I'm in the process of purchasing living quarters for Mom at a community center in Manhattan."

Julia's jaw dropped. "I'm sorry?"

Quentin pointed his thumb back toward The Copperfield House with disdain. "I should have done something like this years ago. Now that Dad's home and putting Mom in the hospital, I feel I have no choice but to take matters into my own hands."

"But... this is Mom's home. She was born on Nantucket.

Heck, even her great-grandfather was born on Nantucket," Julia interjected. "Alana, help me out here."

Alana stared into space, her eyes swelling with emptiness. "I don't know, Julia."

"Julia. Listen to reason," Quentin said, speaking to her the way her financial advisor had when he'd told her to close down the publishing house. "Mom has spent the past twenty-five years living alone in this house. I should say, cursed house. Her health is diminishing. She deserves a new life, whether she knows that or not. Besides, my children and Ella's children live in the city. She can be the grandmother she should have been all this time."

"Should have been? Who are you to say what Mom should have been?" Julia demanded. "Greta Copperfield has always done exactly as she pleased."

"You're talking about another version of our mother, Julia. You're living in the past," Quentin shot. "Am I the only one in this family who's moved on from all this?"

Julia gaped at her brother's words. "I beg your pardon?"

"I don't know. Maybe you're right. Maybe we're not over it." Alana breathed.

"We've all built something for ourselves, Quentin. Just because we're not America's news darling doesn't mean our lives aren't worthy," Julia spat back.

Julia prayed she would never have to confess the failure of her publishing house.

"And what about Dad?" Julia continued. "He's been through hell and back."

"He's the one who put us through hell," Quentin returned. "I thought you of all people believed that? You took off, just the same as I did."

Julia's throat tightened. He spoke the truth.

"Don't tell me that you suddenly believe in this family based purely on this little nostalgic trip home," Quentin continued. "Don't tell me you want to re-open The Copperfield House as some acclaimed artist residency, bring all the poets back in, and pretend like the past twenty-five years didn't happen."

"I'm just saying..." Julia began.

"Let Dad stay here and rot for all I care," Quentin growled. "I, for one, want to take Mom somewhere safe. Somewhere she can start over. And I'm not waiting for any of my sisters to give me the okay to do so."

Suddenly, the screen door between the back patio and the kitchen sprung open to reveal a white-faced Ella.

"Are you crazy?" she hissed. "Mom and I were hardly in the kitchen before you started in on your..."

Greta appeared behind her. A wrinkled hand pressed against the wall for support. Her eyes found Quentin's. For a long moment, Julia expected her to tell him to leave her alone, to let her live out her days at The Copperfield House in peace.

But instead, she exhaled all the air from her lungs and said, "It's not the worst idea I've ever heard."

"Mom... Are you sure about this?" Julia breathed.

Greta took a slight step forward, using all the energy she had left. Ella steadied her mother, her own face tight with worry.

"I'm just so tired," Greta continued. "I don't think I knew how tired I was until your father came home. He made me realize how much of my life I haven't lived. He made me remember a life I'd forgotten. One had loved with my entire heart. He made me realize how much I've lost over the years." She shook her head as her eyes filled with tears. "But he also made me realize that I've had enough. I don't want to live in this house any longer. It's tainted and will never be the way it once was. I don't want to live with all the ghosts of our past. And above all, I do not want to be Bernard Copperfield's wife. Not for one more day."

# Chapter Twenty-Two

How Ella, Julia, and Alana ended up at the Nantucket wine bar along the coastline a little more than an hour after Quentin's outburst, Julia couldn't say. There had been a flurry of angry words, the pronouncement that Quentin "lacked empathy," then the group decision to be quiet to allow Greta to rest, then another outburst before the ultimate exhale that Greta had confessed to wanting out. She wanted a divorce. They had to listen to her.

The three Copperfield sisters sipped wine quietly and watched the ocean lap up against the rocks. Each seemed to stir in their worries.

Julia realized that part of the reason for her sorrows was that, in a way, she'd envisioned The Copperfield House being a savior for her after Jackson's departure and the publishing house's failure.

But ultimately, the Copperfields had already failed twenty-five years ago. They were the walking dead. It was better to get Greta out while they still could.

And maybe Bernard would be happier alone at the house

to eat his cashews and listen to Rachmaninoff. It was a different version of prison. But at least the people who resented him the most, his family, wouldn't lurk down below.

"That night that he tried to cook us dinner..." Julia began thoughtfully. "I feel like he wanted to tell us something."

Alana rolled her eyes. "What could he possibly say? 'I'm sorry for ruining our family.' It's done. Maybe Quentin's right. We should all move on from this. Sell the house. Go back to our lives. Asher's probably waiting for me in Paris, wondering which bakery sells the best baguette... I always know the answer."

"I just think he deserves to be heard," Julia countered, ignoring the Paris comment. "We're all here together for the first time in twenty-five years. And aren't you curious what he might have to say?"

"No," Alana answered, although Julia didn't believe her.

Ella remained lost in thought.

Julia heaved a sigh, lifting her chin toward the sharp and salty winds.

"Do you remember Marcia Conrad? That young woman who—"

"Who Dad was having an affair with," Alana finished. "How could I forget his little blonde sidekick?"

"What about her?" Ella asked softly.

"Well..." Julia groaned, trying to figure out how to explain this without giving up the news that her publishing house was going under. "The other day, I went through those old manuscripts in the downstairs study again. You know, just in case anything stood out to me for the publishing house. I started to look up where some of the writers ended up— in universities and kindergartens, stuff like that. Only Marcia Conrad's career actually took off in a big way."

"That's no surprise," Alana countered. "She was beautiful."

"Her looks have nothing to do with her talent," Ella returned sharply.

"Still," Alana said. "They got her there. Trust me. I worked in that industry for too long."

"Call it curiosity. Call it nosiness. Call it whatever you want. But in any case, I reached out to her to ask her about her time at The Copperfield House," Julia interrupted. "And about the nature of her relationship with our father."

Ella's jaw dropped with surprise. "What! Julia..."

"I figured she wouldn't even see it or that someone from her team would delete it. But instead, I got this crazy email." Julia brought the message from the attorney onto her phone screen, which she showed to Alana and Ella.

"Wow..." Ella breathed.

"Isn't that strange?" Julia demanded. "I mean, why would they react like this? I said in my message that I knew it didn't matter, that I was just trying to put together the pieces of my family's puzzle."

"I don't know if we should put too much stock into this," Alana returned. "Legal teams jump on anything they think might get blown out of proportion. Besides. The girl's smart. She knows to keep her distance from the Copperfield family. We're poison, remember."

Julia's stomach twisted with confusion. Alana was probably right.

Julia sipped the rest of her glass of wine, splayed a ten on the table, and told her silent sisters that she wanted to go for a walk alone to clear her head. It was April 13th, just four days before her forty-third birthday. Had she fantasized about celebrating that birthday with her family in The Copperfield House? Had she pictured her mother baking her a cake? Truthfully, she had, but she now shoved these thoughts deep within her as her stomach tightened with sorrow.

Back to Bartlett. Back to that big house alone.

A divorced friend had tried a dating site called OkCupid for a while with not much success.

Maybe Julia could try her hand at dating for the first time in so long. She pictured herself at a dinner table somewhere, listing her interests one after another as a forty-something accountant sat, bored, across from her.

Ugh.

About five minutes after Julia had escaped the wine bar, she received a phone call from her eldest daughter, Anna.

Julia's heart leaped. At least this was something she understood: how to be a parent to her three most important people.

"Hi, honey," Julia answered. "This is a surprise. How are you doing?"

"Hi, Mom." Anna's voice sounded strained.

"Is there something wrong?" Julia continued to buck forward beneath the April sun, too disengaged from her feelings to understand Anna's.

"Well, Henry said that he stopped by the house, and it looks like nobody's been there in a while? Your SUV's gone?" Anna said. "And then I asked Dad where you might be, and he said he had no idea?"

Julia's stomach twisted strangely. She had to lie her way out of this if only to preserve herself. There was too much going on without this, too, affecting her.

"Oh, honey, your father's been so busy with Beijing stuff that I didn't want to worry him," she explained.

"Yeah? Then where are you? I told Henry maybe you went into Chicago to focus on work."

For a split second, Julia considered saying this was true. But then, what would that lie do for her? Henry would probably try to track her down in the city where he lived, and then she'd be caught.

"I had to head out to Nantucket for the week," Julia explained. "My mother was ill."

The silence on the other end of the line was heavy.

"Your mother?" Anna breathed. "You've hardly ever mentioned your mother. And when we asked about our extended family, you just..."

"I know, honey," Julia replied, her voice laced with exhaustion. "It's all a really long story. I'll tell you one of these days, okay? But I really have to go. Just know that I'm safe. Your dad's safe. We're all good. Keep working hard on your internship. I love you."

"I love you, too." Anna's voice was distrusting and strange.

But before Julia could doubt herself, she hung up the phone. She couldn't worry about her children or her husband or that whole other life just then. She burned with anxiety and stress. She had to walk it off.

Some of the most prominent mansions on Nantucket Island were located on Polpis Road. Years ago, Julia had read an estimate that the entire road and its immense estates were worth upward of four hundred million dollars. This made the eighteen million her father had stolen seem laughable.

As Julia paced down the road, a dog walker approached with five different breeds latched to five different leashes. The dogs were beautiful and gleaming, as though they'd just come directly from the salon. It was a sure bet that they each belonged to a millionaire that lived on Polpis Road, one that was simply too tired to walk them.

Toward the middle of the street, a large, ornate sign read: **PUCK.**

Julia's heart seized with recognition. She'd been to that beautiful red-brick mansion before, played its grand piano, and fell in love with its gleaming staircase railing, which she and Ella had ridden down before Quentin had yelled at them.

The house belonged to Gregory Puck, one of her father's ex-best friends and the man she'd stumbled into at the grocery store when she'd first arrived. The man who'd belittled her and, for the first time, brought up the memory of Marcia Conrad.

What was it he'd said?

*"Gosh, she seemed like such a prop for him, didn't she? While he stole my money right out from under me, she was always right there, performing for us. Distracting us from what he was up to."*

Julia's jaw dropped.

This, together with the email she'd received from Marcia's attorneys, clicked in her mind.

She rushed for the fence that outlined the Puck property, burning with anger. With her finger on the outdoor bell, she heard a loud blare within the mansion. And a moment later, a young man answered it with a simple, "Puck residence."

"Hi. My name is Julia Copperfield. I need to speak with Gregory Puck."

"What is this regarding?"

"Tell him it's urgent," Julia said.

"Mr. Puck is not avail—"

"Hello? Who is that?" Gregory's wife, Bethany, appeared across the vibrant green grass on the lawn that rolled around the mansion. She was stunning in her wide-brim hat and an old-fashioned forest-green dress.

"Hi! Mrs. Puck. It's me, Julia Copperfield."

Bethany's smile flickered in and out as she approached. Confusion filled her eyes. "Julia. Of course. How has your time been on the island?"

She spoke through the fence, reluctant to let Julia in. Maybe she thought she was after the Puck funds, just like her father.

"It's been interesting," Julia replied, sounding cheerful and kind. "I was just on a walk down Polpis Road and remembered you lived right here. Such a beautiful house. We just don't have places as grand as this back in Chicago."

*That's it. All you had to do was compliment rich people to make them melt like butter in your hand.*

"That's very kind of you to say, Julia. I'm sure your place in Chicago is gorgeous, as well. We've always loved Chicago. Gregory goes for the sports. I love the shopping on Michigan Avenue. And the hot dogs!" Bethany giggled playfully.

"Oh, yes. Chicago Dogs are incredible," Julia affirmed.

They exchanged light banter for a few moments, with Julia playing the part of an all-around nice neighbor, not one who was trying to manipulate the conversation in her favor at all.

When the conversation stalled, Julia snapped her fingers and said, "It's so good I ran into you. I've been thinking about what Mr. Puck said at the store."

"Oh, honey. Don't worry about him. He was angry all those years ago, but he's gotten over it. Really. I think he was just taken aback that night at the grocery store. On top of it, he was having a nasty flare-up of back pain."

"Terrible to hear that," Julia offered. "But he has every right to be angry. The question I have is about the young woman he said was always with my father. He couldn't remember her name at first."

"Marcia. Marcia Conrad." Bethany's face became stony. "I remember her well. The men treated her like a trophy, almost passing her back and forth among them."

Julia shook her head disdainfully as though to say, *Men! Can't live with them; can't live without them.*

She then added, "I can't help but think that Marcia might have had something to do with the funds that were stolen from your husband and his friends."

Bethany arched her brow.

"Do you think something like that could have happened?

That maybe Marcia and my father were working together in some way to manipulate your husband?"

Bethany's lips formed a round O. "You know, if that were true, it would answer a lot of questions for me. I couldn't help but wonder why Marcia Conrad bothered to hang around with older men when she could've had anyone she pleased."

Julia's heart jolted against her ribcage. "And if my memory serves me correctly, she left right around the time he was first accused."

"Running away from the mess," Bethany whispered.

Bethany and Julia held the silence for a moment. Overhead, a beautiful long-winged bird streamed toward the clouds above.

"I just can't help but think that she knows something. She's been allowed to have such a promising career while my father's spent the past twenty-five years in prison. Is that strang?"

Bethany turned her eyes to the ground. Together, they stirred in the sorrow and shame that came from learning about a wasted life. Bernard Copperfield had committed crimes, and he'd paid for them, year after year, counting the days. But that didn't mean that Bernard Copperfield wasn't one of the worthiest thinkers of his generation, a man who could have continued to make great and powerful works of literature. All things could be true at once.

"Thank you for your help," Julia said simply. "I have to go."

With that, she turned on her heel and fled down Polpis Road, as though if she remained in the midst of all those mansions for a moment longer, she would suffocate.

# Chapter Twenty-Three

Julia wandered back through downtown, her head stirring with memories of that very last night before everything had changed forever. October 17$^{th}$, 1996. If she remembered correctly, that dinner had been a celebration of Marcia Conrad's early success as a screenwriter. She remembered Marcia's bright light of optimism, her graciousness for Bernard's help, and...

Oh. *Huh.*

Julia stopped short on the sidewalk in front of the post office as another memory sprung to her mind.

Although she'd been embarrassed about it at the time, Julia had allowed Marcia into her inner world of poetry. After that, Marcia had demanded Julia read the poem aloud to everyone at the Copperfield dinner table, citing her as *"the next generation of Copperfield writers."* That had been the very last time Julia had ever read a poem of hers aloud to an audience. Since then, she'd hardly written a creative word herself and had instead allowed herself to feel enthralled with other people's talent and fictional universes.

All the while, Marcia Conrad had worked her way up the ranks of her creative fields, publishing numerous novels, making films, and becoming a successful woman in the entertainment business just like Julia had always longed to be.

Julia's aimless wanderings led her in the front of a warehouse a few streets away from The Copperfield House. Outside, a sign squeaked gently with the breeze.

The sign read:

**BELLOWS FURNISHINGS**

Julia's heart fluttered. A brief wander through her hometown revealed countless ghosts and drummed up so many memories. Here she stood in front of the prosperous business of a man she'd loved with her entire heart and mind.

Did she dare go in?

Julia took a quivering step forward, then used her inertia to force herself to the front door. When she opened it, a chipper secretary in her twenties or thirties greeted her with a bright, "Hello! Welcome to Bellows Furnishings. How can I help you today?"

Somewhere behind the main office came the roar of a machine. Julia could picture Charlie behind it, operating the menacing machinery with artistry and patience. He was always so patient, caring, loyal, and kind.

It was why he'd come back to Nantucket in the first place.

"Hi." Julia tried out her voice and found it shaky. "I was wondering if I could speak to Charlie?"

"If you have any inquiries, you can leave them here with me," the secretary said. "He's really busy during the day, but he checks everything I write to him at night."

In back, the roar of the motor cut out. Julia glanced toward the door between the back room and this front office, daring herself to step forward.

"I just really need to speak to him," she finally protested. "I have a feeling he'll see me."

The secretary arched her brow doubtfully.

"Like I said. He's very busy today, and I've been given strict orders not to interrupt him."

"Charlie?" Julia called. "Charlie. It's me. It's Julia."

The secretary's jaw hung low with surprise. Next came the thunk-thunk-thunk of Charlie's footsteps as he headed for the door. The door flew open to reveal him in just a black tank top and a pair of jeans, dirty from wood shavings and furniture stain.

Just the smell of him, a mix of sweat, wood, and something else, something entirely his own, overwhelmed Julia. She lifted a hand toward the window to whisper, "I just saw the sign and..."

"I told her you like to work throughout the entire day," the secretary informed him. "With no interruptions."

Charlie hardly glanced at the secretary when he said, "Thank you, Hannah. Julia... Would you like to come back?"

Julia had once seen a hilarious TV show that made fun of women who fell in love with carpenters. *"They're so strong and passionate. They can build anything, do anything with their hands,"* the TV show's characters had said. How cliché.

But seeing Charlie in the midst of these gorgeous pieces of furniture nearly shattered Julia.

The pieces were spectacular. There was an armoire with beautifully carved details on every corner. On a commissioned bookshelf, Charlie had engraved the last name of the family it would soon belong to. He was half-done with several desks, which already seemed to glow with the promise of a thousand afternoons reading and writing in front of a window. Julia was wordless.

"You're so talented, Charlie..." she told him when he finished describing the details of a final piece.

"You sound like you're surprised," Charlie said with a laugh.

"No. I always knew you were talented. But these pieces, they're extraordinary. You must be the talk of all the tourists on Nantucket."

"I don't do half-bad," Charlie replied, palming the back of his neck.

Julia gazed longingly at this man, remembering a thousand other afternoons when they'd held hands and talked for hours. What had their conversations even been about? Julia could only remember snippets, beautiful words they'd spoken punctuated with laughing attacks. More than once, Charlie had accidentally shot milkshake out of his nose. It was disgusting.

"Would you like to get dinner with me?" Julia asked finally, piercing through the silence.

Charlie nodded. "I would like that very much. Would you mind waiting about twenty-five more minutes? I just want to wrap this up."

"Of course. I'll go hang out with your secretary. I think she's really taken a liking to me." Julie flashed him a teasing grin.

Charlie's smile widened. "She's very protective of me. I told her that I never wanted outside guests." He then gave a slight shrug as he added, "I'm basically a hermit these days."

Julia nodded. "I can understand why. You've built your own world back here. Why would you want to be involved with anything else?"

* * *

An hour later, Julia and Charlie sat across from one another at Nantucket Calvino's, an Italian place a few blocks from downtown. It had been there for next-to forever, playing host to anniversary dinners and Valentine's celebrations and before-prom dates. Back in their teenage years, Julia and Charlie had daydreamed about having enough money to go there as they'd sat across the street, eating hot dogs in the sunlight.

Julia ordered eggplant parmesan; Charlie ordered lasagna. After years in professional environments back in Chicago, Julia was well-versed in good wines and selected a Primitivo that even made their server say, "Nice choice."

Charlie tilted his head with his wine lifted and said, "Look at us here, Julia. After all this time."

"After all this time," Julia echoed, drawing her wine glass forward to clink with his.

"You've grown up," he told her.

"You haven't," Julia teased.

Charlie laughed, surprised at the joke. He sipped his wine, considering it before nodding with approval. "Sometimes, I really don't think I've done much growing up. I think about the silly kid I was back in the nineties and think, yup, that's still me. But with more wrinkles."

"I think everyone feels that way to an extent," Julia returned. "I try to translate that to my kids— the truth that everyone is making up everything as they go, and nobody really knows what they're doing. But they don't believe me. I'm just their mom."

Charlie laughed good-naturedly. God, she loved his laugh.

"My daughters are the same," he said.

Julia's ears tingled. *Was she jealous? Maybe slightly. Did she have any right to be? Absolutely not.*

"Tell me about your daughters."

"Zoey and Willa. They're twins, which a nightmare back in the early days but really fun later on. My wife and I always said that we blacked out for two or three years or so. We have pictures to prove they were babies and all that, but nothing to prove how miserable we were. Happy, so happy, but so miserable all at the same time, believe it or not."

"Having twins sounds rough," Julia agreed. "My babies

were all born pretty close together—Anna, Henry, and Rachel. For a while, I didn't know where I ended, and they began. But suddenly, so suddenly, they're off building their own lives."

Charlie snapped his fingers. "It happens like that."

"I wish I could go back and see myself during those years," Julia confessed. "I wish I could see myself as a young mother. Was I playful enough? Loving enough? Did I tell enough bedtime stories?"

"Knowing you, Julia, I'm sure you did," Charlie told her. "There was never any doubt in my mind that you would be an amazing mother."

Julia swallowed the lump in her throat. What Charlie had said was very loaded, proof that he'd thought a lot about the fact that they'd wanted to get married and have children and get old together. It just hadn't been in the cards for them.

"Sometimes I can't believe how many good things have happened to me," Charlie continued then when Julia couldn't figure out what to say next. "Sometimes, I ask myself why I deserved so many wonderful things."

Julia laughed. "I've thought that so many times over the years when my children got older and stayed healthy. When my publishing house moved to the Willis Tower."

"My daughters. My furniture business. The fact that I get to go sailing whenever I want." Charlie added.

"How blessed we are," Julia breathed.

They held one another's gaze for a moment. Julia prayed that he wouldn't bring it up again because they'd had to say goodbye all those years ago. She wanted to stay fixated on the happy moments. With all the darkness at The Copperfield House, she wanted to pretend.

The beautiful conversation continued deep into the evening. Charlie told her stories about his daughters, about how Willa was overprotective and Zoey was always concocting a new art project. Julia told him about Rachel's current hatred of the French language and Anna's internship out in Seattle. She told him that Henry was so intelligent that it made her head spin. "Too smart for his own good."

She avoided mention of Jackson. She could hardly admit the divorce to herself.

After dinner, Charlie did something he hadn't done in twenty-five years: he walked Julia back home. Julia shoved her hands in her spring jacket pockets and avoided his gaze, her heart hammering in her chest as they continued to chat about "only the good things," the beautiful memories they had, and all the hopes they had for the future. Namely, Charlie wanted to sail down to the Caribbean; Julia said she'd soon finish her novel. This was a lie. She'd hardly even planned it.

When they reached the sidewalk outside of The Copperfield House, the murmur of voices on the back patio reminded Julia that she'd only escaped the family drama for a little while. It remained there, waiting for her.

"Thank you for a beautiful evening," Julia told Charlie, lifting her eyes toward his. She wanted to memorize his every wrinkle and every laugh line, just in case she couldn't see him again. She wanted to remember the pure happiness of this moment.

In truth, she wanted to throw herself into his arms and sob herself to sleep.

But that wasn't a possibility.

"It was one of the better nights I've had in a long, long time," Charlie told her. After a long pause, he added, "I know Sunday's your birthday."

Julia scuffed her foot against the sidewalk, laughing like a teenage girl. "Forty-three is nothing to celebrate."

"I disagree," Charlie told her. "If anything, tonight taught me there's a lot more to celebrate in this life."

His words felt loaded. Julia's heart dropped into her stomach. The intensity of the air just then brought her eyes up and off to the right, where another set of eyes peered out at them. There he was again: their ghost, Bernard Copperfield. He smoked his pipe thoughtfully, allowing the smoke to billow out toward the clouds above.

He looked like the saddest and loneliest man in the world.

Julia gave Charlie another wave and stepped toward the front porch, her eyes still on her father. When she reached the stoop, the voices from the back patio reached her ears.

It was her mother, in conversation with Ella and Alana.

"Well, you know. He had to get back to the city. His job is important."

"Are you sure you want to move to New York?" Ella asked. "It's a difficult city. Fun to visit... but not always fun to live in."

"We can even set you up somewhere else on the island," Alana suggested.

"Your brother knows best," Greta told them. "I think it's best that I follow his lead."

Julia's throat tightened with sorrow. She glanced up again to find that her father had abandoned his stance in the window, which remained open to allow the springtime breeze to flutter through.

Suddenly, Julia was overwhelmed with understanding.

Her sisters, brother, and mother, were headed forward through time together.

But Julia still needed answers from her father.

Confident after two and a half glasses of wine, Julia stepped through the front door of The Copperfield and headed to the back staircase to find her father.

# Chapter Twenty-Four

Julia pressed her knuckles against the door of her father's upstairs study. Years ago, if you'd found this door closed, the command was clear: Do Not Disturb. Bernard Copperfield, a world-renowned writer, editor, and critic, needed his alone time to stew in his words.

But after two weeks hidden away in his study alone, Julia believed he'd had enough time to stew.

"Dad?" Julia said, her voice girlish and high-pitched with nerves. She rapped her knuckles against the door again, wavering slightly. "Can I speak with you for a moment?"

The footfalls on the other side of the door were heavy. Bernard Copperfield seemed to carry the weight of the world on his shoulders, or at least the weight of his sins. Finally, the doorknob creaked to reveal his burly face, where a mostly-gray and grizzled beard threatened to take full control of his neck.

He looked every bit the hermit he wanted to be.

Only his eyes sparkled with that same sense of curiosity they'd had back in the old days. Julia marveled that you could spend so many years away in prison and still retain that. It seemed against science itself.

"Hi, Dad."

Bernard didn't speak. He stepped back and allowed the door to open wider. Julia entered, surveying the old study. The antique desk stretched out beneath the far window, upon which he'd written his world-renowned classic novel on an old typewriter. An old computer sat off to the right of it, still dusty. Books lined the shelves on both sides of the room, big tomes that carried the weight of philosophers' entire lives' worth of works. It was the very same study Bernard had left behind, save for one detail: he'd brought a single bed into the corner of the room, which had allowed him to live within that space, that tiny cell, for the previous weeks.

One thing surprised Julia even more. The room itself was sparkling clean and organized. Even the tiny bed had been made, probably immediately after he'd gotten out of it.

"I've heard the news," Bernard muttered as Julia clipped the door closed behind her. "I suppose it's for the best."

"About Mom moving to the city, you mean?"

He nodded. "Quentin came up here and informed me that he would be making the arrangements."

"Yes. I'm sorry."

"It's not a problem." Bernard scratched his beard and turned his eyes toward the window. "It's hard to believe that man is the same young boy we raised in this house. He was such a sweetheart." He laughed inwardly, then added, "He hates me more than I even knew it was possible to be hated."

Julia dropped back against the closed door, her heart fluttering in her throat. "If it makes any difference, I don't hate you."

Bernard continued to stare out the window. Julia dropped her gaze toward the desk, where a large stack of printed-out papers sat off to the left, catching the last of the evening sun.

"What's that?" Julia asked. Curiosity moved her toward the pile of papers.

Bernard shrugged. "I had to do something all those years."

Julia considered this an invitation to continue forward, to read the small text at the center of the top page.

**THE TIME HE LOST** by Bernard Copperfield

"It's a novel," Julia said, surprised.

"Yes. It probably still needs a lot of work." He cleared his throat, then added, "I had a lot on my mind the past twenty-five years. I never could have imagined what that time could do to a person. It's difficult to describe with words, but I tried my best with the novel."

Julia thumbed the pages, yearning to flip the title page over and begin to read. This was a passageway into her father's mind during prison. It was priceless.

"I don't blame any of you for wanting to leave me here at The Copperfield House. What happened all those years ago was like a bomb going off. We've been living through the destruction of that ever since."

"Dad..." Julia breathed, searching within herself for something to say. Something that would relieve them both of all that pain.

"I'll make my peace with it," Bernard said. "I have had nothing to live for since I went to prison. And now that your mother's leaving..." He shook his head, heavy with regret.

Julia sensed he was about to ask her to leave. Before he could, she cleared her throat and asked, "Do you mind if I read your novel?"

Bernard scoffed, but not unkindly. "You shouldn't waste your time."

"It's my choice," Julia told him. "And it's important to me."

After a long and aching pause, Bernard nodded. Julia stepped forward and wrapped her hands around the large stack, her heart pounding.

When Julia reached the doorway, she hesitated, then turned back to ask, "Dad... Do you remember Marcia Conrad?"

Bernard stroked his grizzled beard thoughtfully. "Of course I do. She was a gifted young woman, and I've heard she's gone on to do stellar things within the film and literature world. Perhaps that means, in some small way, I've contributed to the art world. But perhaps not."

*Come on. Just ask him. Dig a little deeper, Julia. What do you have to lose?*

"Dad, I don't mean to pry."

Bernard's eyes glittered as he lifted his head. "I imagine you want to ask if we had an affair. Marcia and I."

Julia swallowed the lump in her throat. She suddenly felt like it was her on trial rather than her father.

"Everyone thought that," Bernard offered sadly. "And you can either believe me or not. At this point, I don't care what anyone thinks of me or if they think of me at all. The only thing I can tell you is this. Marcia's writing enthralled me. I adored that she wanted to talk so much about writing and ideas and building an artistic life. Sure, I was forty-five years old and really feeling my age, and perhaps that was part of the reason I allowed the friendship to become so strong. But we never once shared a romantic moment. I was loyal to your mother from the day I met her."

Julia gaped at her father, genuinely shocked at the depths of what he'd just told her.

The only conclusion she could come to was this. Her father had no reason to lie. Not now. Not after twenty-five years in prison.

"I believe you," Julia whispered, genuinely shocked. "I don't know if I should. But I do."

Bernard nodded and dropped into the chair in front of his desk, which looked much emptier after Julia had taken the manuscript away. He fiddled with his pipe, preparing to head to the window for another smoke. Julia stepped into the dark shadows of the hallway and eased the door closed without saying goodbye.

She had no idea what to think now.

All she knew was that her father was a defeated man with nothing to hope for. And that broke her heart.

* * *

Later that night, Julia sat cross-legged on her childhood bed with her laptop digging into her thighs. It was nearing eleven-forty-five, but sleep felt far away and difficult to reach.

Again, Julia searched for Marcia Conrad, zeroing in on her first few projects, including that first indie film she'd worked on out in Los Angeles. The film had been what they'd been celebrating that last night before the accusations came through, the last night before everything had changed.

The film had received several accolades and a smattering of reviews that still remained on the internet, despite having premiered in 1998.

*An intellectual debut from Miss Marcia Conrad.*

*Looking forward to seeing much more from Ms. Conrad.*

*Truly extraordinary to hear a new voice in Hollywood.*

Julia tried to find out how much money it had cost to make that first movie. A million? More? But it had been too long ago; the information was not online.

Was it possible that Marcia hadn't gotten the funding from an outside party? Was there a way to find out?

This "wall" of sorts forced Julia to search for information elsewhere. By midnight, she found herself reading articles about her father's trial, which she'd avoided like the plague back in 1997. Nantucket and all surrounding areas on the east coast had had a field day with the coverage, sending their journalists from all corners to take photographs and write articles about the "Genius Who Conned His Friends Out Of Millions."

She read:

*Through a series of embezzlements, bad checks, and lies, Bernard Copperfield stole upward of eighteen million dollars from his dearest islander friends.*

*Bernard Copperfield, swindler extraordinaire.*

*Bernard Copperfield knew the nature of his friends' bank accounts and connections. And he used his know-how to take all he could.*

As Julia continued to read into the night, she realized that many of the journalists had focused on the more social aspects of the trial, the social status of the people who'd been stolen from, along with the ramifications on island life in general. *"Who Can We Trust?"* a Nantucket journalist had written in February 1997, just three months before Bernard had been sentenced.

Just when Julia was about to give up her search, she discovered a strange keyword that no other article had mentioned previously.

*Today, the jury pores over email records between Bernard and his ex-friends, which prove the lengths of manipulation Bernard was willing to go to.*

"Email records?" Julia murmured out loud.

Julia then went to the search bar to type "email records, Bernard Copperfield trial." Only two other articles came up, briefly mentioning "email records." Had the trial happened in modern times, there probably would have been screenshots of the email records themselves.

Still, this proved something beyond a shadow of a doubt.

Bernard Copperfield was the least tech-savvy person Julia knew. Back in the nineties, he'd been resistant to all things that involved the internet. He'd hated the computer they'd set up in his study, saying it was a monstrosity and an "attack on all literature."

The fact that they'd thought he had an email was laughable.

*Why hadn't he disputed that?*

Julia dropped her head back on the pillow, her mind whirring. This "email" thing wasn't proof that Marcia had been involved. But it did make Julia think that Bernard wasn't totally to blame.

Plus, Marcia Conrad had been his permanent shadow during the time that he'd stolen all these funds. It was more than suspicious.

But it would be very difficult to prove anything, especially so long after the case had closed.

# Chapter Twenty-Five

When Julia headed downstairs the following morning for a cup of coffee, she discovered Ella hovering between the front porch and the foyer, carrying a large stack of boxes.

"Are you stuck?" Julia called, taking the stack of boxes and pulling them the rest of the way through the door.

Ella sighed with relief. As Julia placed the boxes next to the couch, Ella removed her boots and leather jacket, explaining that she and Alana had gone out to pick up moving boxes and breakfast donuts for the day ahead.

"We talked it over with Mom," Ella explained. "And we want to help her get set up for her new life."

Julia nodded, her stomach twisting. *How could she explain what she'd learned last night without sounding like a lunatic? It had all been twenty-five years ago. Why couldn't she let it go?*

Alana appeared in the doorway, carrying a white cardboard box from the local donut shop. She smiled wearily as she removed her tennis shoes with the flip of her toes. *What had she done with her expensive heels?* Besides that, she now wore a big Nantucket Volleyball sweatshirt, which had probably been locked away in her wardrobe since she'd left for the city.

She looked like the Alana that Julia remembered from before.

The authentic Alana.

"Donuts, anyone?" Alana sang it as she stepped toward the kitchen. "I've been craving a baguette, but these will have to do."

"Just when I think she's our Alana, she reminds me that she's actually *'Alana in Paris'*..." Ella whispered under her breath, alluding to the Netflix show Emily in Paris.

"What are you girls talking about in there?" Alana called.

Despite everything, Julia laughed and joined her sisters in the kitchen, grateful for a moment of normalcy. She sunk her teeth into a cream-filled donut and listened as Ella talked about the old donut shop.

"It still has that same guy behind the counter," she said. "He was about a million years old when I left the island, and now, I guess he's about..."

"Four million," Alana affirmed. "With a nice little donut belly."

"That's how you know his product is good," Ella said. "He indulges every now and again. As he should."

Ella and Alana discussed their strategy for the day ahead.

"Mom's already told us she wants to get rid of almost everything," Ella explained. "But I think that's easier said than done. She's lived here for decades, and this place is swimming in memories. And every trinket, every painting, every corner will require some conversation."

"You're right," Alana agreed. "And all that's without mentioning the stuff we might like to have. Did you hear Quentin before he left? He wants to bring someone in to appraise how much everything is worth."

"Typical that the guy with more money than God wants to take account of every penny," Ella breathed.

Julia was grateful for her sisters' straightforward approach but still felt reticent and unsure.

"When do you plan on getting started?" Julia asked.

"As soon as Mom's ready," Ella recited.

"My guess is she'll take one look at the boxes and say she needs more time," Alana offered.

"Oh, God. You're probably right," Ella said with a laugh.

And in fact, Alana was very right.

The stack of boxes terrified Greta. She didn't say it outright but simply made an excuse as to why she couldn't begin to pack that day, pressing her hand against her lower back and complaining about "back problems." Alana and Ella exchanged glances while Julia watched on, her arms crossed tightly over her chest.

"We can try to do this all in your own time, Mom," Ella suggested. "I'm not sure when Alana and Julia have to get going, but I can stay here as long as you like."

"I still have a bit of time," Alana affirmed. "Julia?"

"Oh. Um." Julia stirred with panic. "I've just been working remotely, which reminds me. I have to head upstairs to work on some stuff."

"Sure. We'll come to get you if we need you!" Alana called as Julia scampered up the steps.

The manuscript Julia had taken from her father sat on the desk beneath the window, presenting a daunting task. As her book revenue streams depleted and agents hardly contacted Orchard Publishing any longer, Julia felt at a loss— yet hungry to dig her teeth into the text again.

She didn't expect to love her father's newest work.

His Prison Opus.

But the moment Julia sat down with the one-hundred and twenty-five thousand-word text, her heart lifted into her throat, filled with expectation and promise.

Unlike so many other texts from novice writers she'd read over the past few years, her father's text was articulate and thoughtful. He moved through emotions and conversations with ease and grace. At no point in the text did Julia lose track of where she was or where she had been. And within the first hour of reading, she'd begun to root for the main character.

The first quarter of the book focused on the daily life of an inmate in prison, not unlike the one her father had spent his time in. There was the achy boredom, the friendships, the bickering, and the all-out wars. The writing eased you into the mindset of that life without apologizing for it or making you feel bad for the character.

Around thirty-five thousand words into the text, her father dropped a bomb:

The novel's main character hadn't actually done the crime he was serving time for.

And through his day-to-day life in prison, he struggled with the reality of knowing he hadn't done the crime, alongside the knowledge that everyone he'd ever loved absolutely hated him.

Julia lifted her eyes from the text as her heart pounded.

*Was it possible that the real Bernard Copperfield was innocent?*

This was a fictional work, Julia told herself. Even if he was innocent (not that she could prove that at the moment), this novel wouldn't sway anyone's opinion of him.

But...

If she played her cards right...

The novel could be used in a very different way.

Julia continued to read, beginning to make notes to herself as she went along. Bit by bit, the main character's story stopped resembling Bernard's life so much and took on a story of its own. When a new guard accidentally kills an inmate, the main character takes the fall for the killing... which results in his placement on death row.

The move struck Julia as both painful and understandable.

In a diary entry the main character wrote, he scribed this:

*The young man is a murderer, yes. But he has a wife, two children, and a dog.*

*What do I have to come home to?*

*Even when they release me in ten years' time, my children won't be there, waiting for me. My wife hasn't contacted me in years. The love we once shared is now a sort of dream-like memory. It's difficult for me to remind myself that that was, in fact, a reality. For a brief time, I had it all.*

Julia continued to read and reread the manuscript into the late evening, ignoring Alana and Ella's calls to come down for dinner with Greta. At eight-thirty, she found herself calling her financial advisor, Randy, to tell him, "We're staying in the publishing game a little bit longer, and I'm throwing a Hail Mary."

"Julia. Please. Listen to reason."

But Julia wouldn't listen to reason. She'd already lost too much.

Julia's editor and marketer had been lying in wait to hear from Julia. When she finally reached out to them that night, they immediately jumped on a video call with her to discuss the potential book. Julia didn't give away the writer's name but talked about the "promising voice," the "relatable tale of loss," and "a story about prison life that the world needs right now."

"Empathy for prisoners," her editor said, nodding as she jotted something on her pad of paper. "I can buy that."

"I think a lot of people would buy it," her marketer affirmed. "Let's get cracking on this. Set up a meeting with the writer. ASAP."

Julia's throat tightened. "I'll get back to you on that," she replied.

Julia stayed up late that night, jotting down notes and scribing a letter to her father, one that would help her highlight her points about why the novel deserved to be published and where she saw the editing process going. "It could be great, Dad," she muttered to herself. "I'll be your editor. You, the writer. We could work together for the first time."

It was easier said than done, she knew. But she had to hold out hope. What else did she have?

# Chapter Twenty-Six

That Friday afternoon, Julia and Ella drove out to Manakuket Beach on the western shore. They splayed a blanket across the chilly sands, wrapped up in sweatshirts and flannels, and watched in silence as the waves rolled toward them, cresting and then casting froth across the sand. Julia had spent all morning engrossed in her father's words, making notes and writing with her marketer about potential plans.

Beside her on the blanket, Ella seemed lost in her own deep thoughts.

"Do you remember when we used to have family picnics out here?" she asked suddenly, her voice hardly penetrating the howling winds.

"Yes. Dad would load up the van and guide the artists from the house to the beach, where we'd set up an all-day camp. Bonfires. Singing songs. Eating in the sun and then rushing into the water." Julia whispered, lost in the memory.

"I sometimes wonder if I made a mistake not giving my children the beauty of growing up here," Ella murmured.

"We all had to get away," Julia returned. "At least, that's what I tell myself. To shove away the guilt."

Ella nodded, her eyes glowing.

"I think I had to forgive myself a long time ago for leaving you and Mom behind," Julia whispered then. "Otherwise, I might have destroyed myself with anger at myself. I'm sorry, so sorry. But that doesn't mean that you have to forgive me. I only wish you would."

"We're in our forties, now, Julia," Ella breathed. "We shouldn't carry any anger, guilt, or shame from that time. Not anymore. It's been too long."

Julia and Ella shared the silence for a long time. Julia's stomach stirred with confusion. They'd all returned to The Copperfield House to see it through to the bitter end. *But what happened next between Julia, Ella, and Alana? Would they go back to not speaking?*

A rain spit out from the rolling clouds above. Julia and Ella clambered to their feet, wrapped up the blanket, and headed back to Julia's SUV. Ella mentioned getting back to the city, as her part-time jobs would probably let her go soon if she didn't return. Julia nodded at the logistics, even though they seemed so sterile. "I keep telling Mom I have all the time in the world. Maybe I do. I can always get another stupid part-time job."

Julia turned the SUV down the road that led to their old home. Slowly, they crept past the old homesteads and headed straight for the glowing ocean at the far end of the street. Julia then parked and stared straight ahead, her eyes toward the frothing waters.

Moments later, Ella interrupted her serene reverie.

"What are those teenagers doing here?" Ella asked.

For a moment, Julia thought she'd entered a nightmare.

When she followed Ella's gaze, she found three very familiar figures before her— each with a backpack across their back, wearing stoic expressions. They stared at the SUV earnestly, waiting for the people within to get out.

It was Anna, Henry, and Rachel.

"Those are... those are my kids," Julia whispered, her voice rasping.

With a huge surge of energy, Julia leaped out of the SUV and stepped toward her three children, toward Henry, who might as well have been Jackson's twin, toward her headstrong and creative Anna, and toward her baby, Rachel. *What were they doing here? How had they found her?*

Ah. Of course. Julia had mentioned Nantucket to Anna on the phone the other day.

There came the sound of Ella opening and closing the passenger door of the SUV. All the while, Julia stood out on the grass as a Nantucket April rain continued to pour down upon them.

Finally, Anna spoke.

"When were you going to tell us?" she demanded.

Ella appeared beside Julia, trying on a smile that fell off just as quickly. "Hello, you three. My name is Ella."

"Aren't you the lead singer of Pottersville?" Henry asked, his eyes widening.

Even Ella's laughter was musical. "You can also just call me Aunt Ella."

Henry's eyes traced from Julia to Ella, back to Julia. Confusion lined his face.

"Don't drop the subject," Anna blared, her eyes trained on Julia.

Above, the second-floor study window opened wider to reveal one-half of Bernard Copperfield's grizzled beard. Pipe smoke billowed out. He was eavesdropping on the drama that was about to unfold.

Ella glanced toward Julia, arching her brow. "Why don't we all go inside?"

Julia nodded, shellshocked. She stepped toward her children, who parted like the Red Sea and allowed her to enter the house. Once in the foyer, she removed her shoes and ruffled her jet-black hair.

"There you are," Greta greeted gently from the corner, where she hovered over a half-packed box of books. "I can't believe it, but I'm finally getting a few things together."

After Julia, came her children, like a line of baby ducks, one after another. When Anna appeared, Greta's lips parted with genuine surprise. When Rachel and Henry joined them, Greta draped a hand across her cheek. She stood on thin legs, wordless, and her eyes shone with a love that had no bounds.

"Your children. Julia... Your children are here."

Julia's heart dropped into her belly like a stone. Anna, Henry, and Rachel looked at their mother with a mix of confusion and curiosity.

Julia introduced them with soft tones. "This is my eldest, Anna. This is Rachel. And this..."

"Must be Henry," Greta finished her sentence. She stepped around the boxes, her arms lifting up coaxingly. She wanted to give them a hug but seemed not to know how.

Rachel sniffled, then dabbed the corners of her eyes with the edge of her sleeve. When a sob escaped her, she apologized and said, "I'm sorry. I hardly slept last night. I'm just so..."

"Why don't I make everyone some tea," Greta offered kindly. She touched Rachel's upper arm and guided her toward the kitchen. Henry stepped after them, glowering at Julia.

This left only Julia, Ella, and Anna in the living room, the air heavy around them.

"Your father told you," Julia finally spoke. She ran a hand through her hair as she stole a glance at her oldest.

"He told Henry," Anna corrected. "When I talked to you on the phone the other day, you sounded completely unlike yourself. I told Henry to push Dad for the truth. Dad was always more candid with Henry. A guy thing, I guess."

Julia dropped onto the edge of the couch, pressing her knuckle into her chin. She could barely look at her daughter, could only sit and stew in Anna's rage and sorrow.

"I learned about Beijing the same day you kids did," Julia stated.

"What? Beijing?" Ella's voice was high-pitched.

"Are you kidding me?" Anna demanded. "He didn't tell his own wife?"

Julia shook her head, splayed her hands over her eyes, and pressed onto them until she saw only spots. "Your father's career has skyrocketed in the past few years. It's not that I'm not happy for him. It's not that I don't think he deserves it. It's just that... He wants something else now. The life we had together in Bartlett, one he chose, is something he doesn't what anymore. Meanwhile, the publishing house..."

Julia couldn't bring herself to say it. She couldn't begin to describe the Hail Mary she was now throwing if only to save the only thing she'd ever built herself.

Anna sat beside her mother and gently placed a hand across her upper back. Ella wrapped a hand over hers. Together, they sat in silence in the shadows of the living room, waiting for something to happen.

"You should have said something," Ella whispered.

"I just did what I knew best," Julia murmured. "I tried my best but then ran."

A wail swelled out of the kitchen. Julia shot up in protective mode for her youngest daughter. As she headed for the kitchen, the sobs escalated.

There in the kitchen, Rachel huddled in the corner, her hands wrapped around her elbows and her face blotchy. Her cries were loud and all-consuming; her body shook with the weight of her emotions. Across the kitchen, Greta and Henry looked on, both at a loss. The kettle on the stovetop began to scream with a similar rage.

"Honey…" Greta breathed.

Julia tried to step toward her youngest daughter, but the sight of Julia made Rachel reach meltdown mode. Poor girl, in the first year of her university career, struggling through French and asking herself all these questions about her life. Now, she stood in her mother's childhood home. Little did Rachel know that the place was now filled with such ugly history and marred Julia's childhood happiness.

It was such a funny picture, despite how sad it was.

Because actually, Julia couldn't remember when any of the Copperfields had cried like this— with their entire bodies, hearts, and souls. Instead, they'd taken on what had happened twenty-five years ago and ignored it, refusing to talk about it. This had made the pain that much more monstrous, growing silently, like cancer.

"I just don't know why you couldn't just…" Rachel heaved, unsure of where she wanted the sentence to go.

"Just be happy?" Julia asked. "Just go with your father wherever he wanted to go? Just force myself to align with his every whim?"

Rachel hiccupped and cried harder. Julia closed her eyes tightly as a headache swelled in the back of her skull. When she opened them again, she found Henry giving her a dark look.

"This is a hell of a way to learn that our family is breaking up," Henry told her pointedly. "Very adult of you."

Twenty-five years after the collapse of her first family, Julia found herself in that same house, in the midst of another catastrophe. *How could she explain to Henry that she'd never really grown up? That she'd never escaped her demons from The Copperfield House? That she was just a frightened middle-aged woman without a clue?*

Back in the living room, there came the twinkling sound of the baby grand piano. All the hair on the nape of Julia's neck stood up straight at the sound. Although the baby grand hadn't been tuned in what sounded like a few years, the sound was nostalgic and utterly beautiful. After a brief moment of broken and blissful chords, the piano player transitioned to one of Julia's favorite classical pieces— Rachmaninoff's Rhapsody on a Theme of Paginini.

As the music welled over them, not an eye in the kitchen of the house remained dry. Rachel's manic crying had stopped, and she stood, rapt with attention, her cheeks blotchy and red. Across the kitchen, Greta pressed an entire Kleenex against both eyes, wanting to hide out from the world and experience only the sound of this purely nostalgic tune.

It was time to greet their musical genius.

It was time to end the madness.

Bernard Copperfield sat at the piano bench in the next room, his eyes half-open as his fingers fluttered over the keys. Julia stood in the far corner of the room, clutching her heart, as her three children saw her father, the once-lost Bernard, with his grizzled beard and his sagging cheeks and that same-old twinkle in his eyes. Ella, too, wiped her eyes, seemingly unable to even look at their father.

Greta joined the group last, dropping into the antique armchair in front of the bay window and taking in the splendor of the man she'd once loved and lost.

The entire house was quiet when the song finished, save for the subtle creaks brought on by the Atlantic winds. Bernard's eyes scanned the keys. He seemed too frightened to look up at them and acknowledge what he'd done.

But finally, he drummed up the strength to speak.

"We've lost so much in this family—so much time. And I'm not sure if any of that pain ever adds up to anything," he began.

A sob escaped Greta's lips. She stared at the half-packed box of books despairingly.

"I can't speak for my wife, Greta. But I can say it's a joy to have my daughter Julia's children here with us. Regardless of the circumstances, I'd like to sit with you and know you, as best as I can, with all the time we have."

# Chapter Twenty-Seven

I t was fresh off the jagged mess of that afternoon that the Copperfields gathered around the back patio table with a large stack of pizzas, two liters of soda, and several bottles of red wine from a local Nantucket winery. Rachel's face remained blotchy with sorrow; Henry remained surly; and Anna's eyes bugged out with a mix of curiosity and distrust, eyeing her Aunt Ella, her grandmother, and her grandfather suspiciously. Julia didn't have the strength to patch everything up. She wasn't the "super mom" she'd been back in the old days. She'd had enough.

After another long stretch of silence, Ella opened the top box of pizza and asked the Crawford children, "How did you find us here?"

Anna took a small sip of wine. Both of her siblings turned to her for the answer. "Our dad said that Mom was on Nantucket somewhere and that she'd never told him exactly where she'd grown up. But I did some light internet research and..." She gestured toward the Victorian home behind her. "There's a whole lot of stuff online about The Copperfield

House. Like, blogs and documentaries and articles and..." Anna's eyebrows rose. "This place was beloved by so many writers and artists and musicians."

"Yes, it really was," Greta murmured thoughtfully.

Bernard stared down at his empty plate. It was strange to see him seated amongst them, his shoulders pushed forward and his chin toward his chest. He was broad and muscular, like a man of the woods rather than a man of words.

It went without saying that Anna's research had led her to the story of Bernard Copperfield and the trial that had torn their family apart forever. She gave her grandfather a curious look, edged with pain.

Julia itched to tell her children. The mess of her life was laid out on a platter. She was done with hiding the truth and telling white lies.

"Anyway. That's how I found the address," Anna finished. "We all bought flights to Boston and managed to get to Hyannis this afternoon in time for the ferry."

It was a strange thing imagining Julia's three children reaching the Hyannis bus station. This was where the adventure of Julia's life had begun, It was as though they'd "tracked her down."

Even more surprising was the fact that Julia didn't care any longer. This was her life, and the people at the table were her greatest loves. The fact that she'd run away from her problems for so long was laughable. It was time to grow up.

Again, silence. They reached for slabs of pizza, eating slowly as the sun dropped toward the western horizon. Bernard waited to be served last, watching everyone else with sharp eyes to make sure they were well-fed. Just as he reached for a slice of pepperoni, the back door opened to reveal Alana, all five-foot-nine of her, with beautiful Chanel sunglasses and jet-black skinny jeans.

"Honey, I'm home!" Alana cried. Almost instantly, the realization of what she'd just walked into played out over her face. The corners of her lips wiggled with confusion. "This is quite a group." She arched an eyebrow toward their father, who bowed his head and stared at his pepperoni pizza.

"Our time here is running out," Ella said suddenly. "So, Dad thought it would be a great idea to spend as much of that time together as we can."

"All of us, save for Quentin," Greta added. "He's just so busy in the city."

"How many Copperfields are there?" Henry joked. "You keep coming out of the woodwork."

Everyone at the table laughed appreciatively, grateful for the distraction. Julia introduced Aunt Alana to her three children, who she greeted warmly as she flipped off her expensive sunglasses. "Your girls are stunning, Julia," she complimented.

"They're pretty dang smart, too," Julia added proudly.

"Mom..." Rachel moaned.

"All Copperfields are intelligent," Bernard said suddenly. "Ironically, they get their cleverness from Greta, who wasn't actually born a Copperfield. She just does everything better than me, is all. You should have read some of the short stories she published. People couldn't get enough of her words. Remember, Greta?"

Greta's cheeks burned red as another bout of silence surrounded them. The glance Bernard gave her was glittering with promise and love.

Perhaps this was the way forward, Julia thought.

Perhaps this was the forgiveness they needed to keep going.

Even with Greta off to NYC, it was important for Bernard and Greta to honor the past. Their love had once been powerful. It had once meant the world.

Toward the end of dinner, Ella tilted her head and said, "You know, we have a big family event happening on Sunday."

"Oh, goodness me." Greta smacked her hands over her cheeks. "I have so much shopping to do."

Bernard's eyes sparkled knowingly. "Forty-three, isn't it?"

Julia blushed, trying to shove her tears back.

"We haven't celebrated your birthday since you turned seventeen," Alana whispered. "It was right before I went to NYC with Asher. I was so nervous at the time. I remember I could hardly eat the birthday cake Mom made you."

"I guess we'd better have a proper Copperfield birthday party," Greta said, eyeing Rachel adoringly. "Maybe you could help me make your mother a birthday cake?"

"That sounds lovely," Rachel returned, perking up. "She loves carrot cake."

"Oh, I know she does," Greta offered. "She always has. I made her a carrot cake every year from her twelfth birthday on. And she always ate at least two pieces, and sometimes three."

"We know." Anna, Henry, and Rachel said this all at once, exchanging funny glances.

"Hey!" Julia cried playfully. "Not every year!"

"Every year," Anna affirmed. "But we like it. Birthdays were always a big deal at our house."

"Ours, too," Ella told her thoughtfully.

Julia glanced toward Bernard, whose eyes continued to bore through his pizza. This was probably too much socializing at one time, too many conversations to keep track of, and too many people he'd never known.

"One more birthday at The Copperfield House," Greta murmured, mostly to herself. "Yes. It has to be done."

* * *

Later that night, after Greta had gone to bed, Alana and Ella sat around the table with their newfound nieces and nephew, swapping stories from their separate pasts, sipping wine, and eating snacks. Julia watched them from the doorway, her heart swelling with love. At one point, Alana told a silly story about a young Julia's wardrobe malfunction at a school dance, which made all three of Julia's children howl with laughter.

"You guys have to hear this song," Rachel said excitedly, turning on her Bluetooth speaker to play a rock song that she reported, "everyone in college is obsessed with."

"It's cool..." Ella replied, lifting her hands to play air guitar. "Really cool, actually. It reminds me of some of the bands I used to tour with in the 'oos."

"Gosh, I want to pick your brain about that." Henry began, starstruck. "Tour stories. Other bands you met. I mean, did you ever hang out with Jack White?"

Ella laughed. "That guy? Let's just say he was difficult. Will never really liked him."

"Will. Right. He's also in the band," Henry noted. "And you two have kids, right?"

"Two." Ella's smile was far away. "Danny and Laura. They're eighteen and seventeen years old. I'd love for you to meet them sometime. Maybe in the city, after we move your grandmother to her new home."

Julia stepped out of the kitchen and sat in the shadows of the hallway, suddenly exhausted. Her children carried on talking to their aunts without her, probably assuming she'd stepped upstairs to sleep.

"I can't believe this huge house has been sitting here empty, well, partially empty all this time," Anna breathed. "We had no idea about any of you. Mom hardly ever spoke about her past."

"I feel like it's our fault for not asking," Rachel suggested.

Her children shared this silence for a long time until Alana broke it.

"When Dad went to prison..." she began. "It destroyed all of us in different ways. The Copperfield family exploded into nothing. Your mother's not the only one who didn't talk about it. I can name maybe three people in my life I've told the story to."

"Did you tell your children?" Henry asked Ella.

"They don't know everything," Ella explained. "Your grandmother helped here and there when Will and I went on tour, so they grew up knowing this house and the island."

"Wow. I would have loved to know this place." Anna breathed.

"What's going to happen to it when Grandma moves to New York City?" Henry asked.

"We haven't talked about the logistics," Ella explained.

"But we think your grandfather will probably remain here," Alana offered.

"Alone?" Rachel asked, aghast. "After all that time in prison? He'll have to live out the rest of his days... alone?"

Nobody seemed to know what to say. Julia's stomach twisted; she nearly vomited up her dinner. Rachel had echoed the sentiment that Julia had sat with for the past several days. *How could they leave their father alone?*

Of course, Julia had information that the rest of her siblings didn't have.

Careful not to be spotted by her children, Julia headed up the back staircase and again knocked on the door of her father's study. His "come in" was gentle, as though she was eight years old again, ready with a question about the stars, moon, or ocean.

Bernard remained poised at the window with his chin lifted as the breeze fluttered through his beard. He looked poetic there at the window, still trapped in his personal prison and unwilling or unable to get out.

"Thank you for what you did earlier," Julia said as she clicked the door closed. "I've never seen my daughter like that."

Bernard nodded firmly. There was a long silence before he said, "Your children are beautiful, Julia. They're kind and considerate. And I think they came all this way because they were worried about you."

Julia dropped down on the side of the bed, bouncing slightly. From this perspective, a large moon rose out from beyond the window, hovering just over Bernard's head.

"I hate that they're worried about me," Julia breathed. "But I guess I haven't given them much reason to believe in me. Especially now that their father has left us, and my publishing house is..."

Bernard finally turned back, eyeing her without judgment. "They look at you with all the love in the world, Julia. I remember when my four children used to look at me like that. I don't think I'll ever get it back."

Julia's throat tightened with surprise. She pulled her shoulders back, forcing herself to stay present and not fall back into silence and despair.

"I read your novel. I read it once, and then I had to go back and read some sections over and over again because I just couldn't get enough."

Bernard didn't dare look at her.

"It's beautiful, Dad. It's one of the most stunning pieces of literature I've read in years."

*What could it mean to a once-renowned novelist to hear that he hadn't lost his touch? What could it mean to him that the time in prison wasn't for nothing?*

A tear traced Bernard's cheek before joining the thick strands of his beard. "I don't know what to say." He sniffed, continuing. "For years, I was nothing except the words I put on that page. Now that it's actually been read... It's like someone else lived part of those years with me. It's like you saw who I was during the hardest times of my life."

"It's a difficult thing to imagine," Julia whispered. "Day in, day out."

"For twenty-five years," he said. "All the while, I missed

this house, this island, the ocean, the trees... And most desperately, my family. My Greta." He closed his eyes for a long time. His breaths came, jagged and sharp. "And now that I've come back, I don't have the strength to fix anything. We're broken beyond repair. I'll have to spend the rest of my life regretting that."

His words were impenetrable. They felt like a closed door.

"I have to ask you something, Dad," Julia said.

Bernard nodded once, his eyes toward the moon.

"I wanted to know if you'd allow my publishing house to publish your novel," Julia continued. "I believe it's a really beautiful and poignant work of fiction, something that people should read. It's been years since they had your first book in their hands, and you owe it to them to see what that mind of yours has been up to all these years."

"I don't know, Julia. It's one thing to show the manuscript to you. It's another to release it to the world and listen to them ridiculing me all over again," Bernard began.

Julia pressed her lips together, anxious about what she knew she had to say next.

"Dad. You're the only person on earth who could tell this story."

Bernard lifted his eyes toward hers. Together, they shared a moment of complete understanding.

"Are you saying what I think you're saying?" Bernard breathed.

"There are too many things that don't add up," Julia whispered. "Too many things I can't understand about the case. And then I read this book, digging into its emotion, marveling at how real this sorrow feels..." She shook her head in awe. "Dad. Are you innocent?"

Bernard rubbed a red spot at the bridge of his nose with a finger that looked craggy and old. *How had that felt, watching himself age with time in that terrible place?*

"I gave up saying I was innocent," Bernard finally admitted. "Nobody believed me. Not your mother. Not you kids. Not my friends. And the money was gone. It was gone from their accounts, and I was the only link to all of it. It made no sense. They pulled out all this proof against me, stuff I didn't recognize at all."

"The emails..." Julia whispered.

"What did I know about emails in 1996?" Bernard demanded. "I hated technology. Still hate it today. These phones you and your sisters are carrying around... They're like mini-computers! Why do you have to stay connected to the outside world so much? What happens to your creative mind? What happens to your dreams?"

Julia shook her head. "As a culture, I think we've stopped paying attention to dreams and given all our attention to memes."

Bernard's eyes widened. "What in the heck is a meme?"

Julia shook her head, suppressing laughter. None of this was funny, not in the least. But her nerves were skyrocketing.

"I want to help prove that you're innocent, Dad," she told him firmly. "And I think one of the first steps to do that is publishing this book. Tell me. Are you willing to work hard with me, rewrite and edit every step of the way until the book is cleared for publication? Are you willing to bare your soul for your avid readers one last time?"

Bernard sent his answer back toward the moon. It seemed too difficult for him to meet Julia's eyes.

"What do I have to lose?"

# Chapter Twenty-Eight

Exactly twenty-five years after she and Charlie had celebrated her eighteenth birthday in Central Park, Julia awoke and found herself to be forty-three years old— and ready for a divorce. She stood in the shadows of the bathroom down the hall, inspecting her face, her dyed-black hair, her still-plump lips, and the little wrinkles that tightened around the outer part of her eyes. She then raised her left hand ceremoniously and inched the wedding band and engagement rings off her fourth finger. Life was about rituals, after all. And this felt like the first step toward the rest of her life.

Julia waved her fingers to-and-fro to feel the strangeness of her naked finger, which seemed light and free. It was time.

Back in her old bedroom, Julia paced as she got on the phone with a friend-of-a-friend who'd helped a few acquaintances through their divorces. "She's the best because she's been through one herself," a publishing friend had said. "Cutthroat and takes no prisoners. That kind of thing."

To Julia's surprise, the divorce attorney answered the phone herself (without the assistance of a secretary) on the second ring and set up a meeting for the following week to go over more details of Julia's particular case. When she learned that Julia's husband was Jackson Crawford, the rising-star journalist from Chicago who'd just gone out to Beijing, she laughed outright.

"Men always think they can run off and rule the world," she said. "But you'll make him remember what he's lost."

"I don't even think I care about that," Julia told her thoughtfully, watching as the sunlight glowed through the east-side window. "I just want to be free of him, and I want our entire story to end."

"The minute you want to be free, it's over," the attorney told her. "Because it means he no longer has any power over you. It's a beautiful thing."

With the ring off her finger and the morning at her disposal, Julia dressed in a pair of shorts, a sports bra, and a sweatshirt. She slipped her feet into a pair of tennis shoes and hustled out the door. Besides a brief athletic stint in her thirties, Julia hadn't done much of any running in years. However, on the morning of her forty-third birthday, her legs stretched out beautifully before her, reminding her of a gazelle. Sweat flickered across the front and back of the sweatshirt before pooling out, dampening everything. She sucked in a breath and then released it as she continued to sprint down the beach, her eyes toward the waves and the wide-open sea.

It was a glorious thing to feel so alive.

It was a glorious thing to be given a fresh start.

She stopped at the edge of the seaside, flung her fists back behind her, and cried out across the ocean, screaming with all the power in her lungs, heart, and stomach. The sound seemed to sweep across the ocean without returning. It was therapeutic to hear the sound of her pain. It was therapeutic to let it out.

During Charlie and Julia's walk from his furniture warehouse, he'd pointed out where he'd raised his daughters, there on Lincoln. Unnerved by change and her frantically beating heart, Julia raced the rest of the way to Lincoln, where she paused in front of the two-story home and shifted her weight from foot to foot. The willow tree in the front yard wept and fluttered with the soft breeze.

*Charlie would think she was a crazy person if he saw her like this.*

*Wouldn't he?*

But hadn't he seen her through so many different levels of crazy back in the day— and accepted her, despite it all?

Hadn't he been the only one in her life to ever truly "get her"?

Before she knew it, she appeared before the front door and rapped her knuckles frantically. The sight of his face, even now, was like medicine, and she needed it.

Charlie answered the door wearing a t-shirt and a pair of sweatpants. He wore a five o'clock shadow across his strong chin, and the smell of musk that lingered around him was intoxicating. Julia's heart surged with love for him. She could have just jumped him right then and there, with the door open for all the neighbors to see. *Do you want Nantucket gossip? I'll give you Nantucket gossip.*

"Julia..." Charlie whispered, his eyes playing out a mixture of happiness and surprise. "What are you..."

"Charlie, I'm divorcing my husband. It's been over for a long, long time."

Charlie's lips parted with surprise. He held her gaze, his eyes filled with longing.

"Julia..."

"Don't try to talk me out of it," Julia continued, stuttering and gasping, miserable after sprinting all that way.

"No. Julia..."

"Because my children are here already. They know. We're all going to move forward together. I'm going to start being honest with them about my past, who I was and who I want to be. And my father's new manuscript, it's brilliant, Charlie. My publishing house will release it, and it will be our saving grace for him, our family and my publishing house. It's the only thing I ever built with my own two hands and I'm not going to let it fail like my marriage."

Julia stretched her palms out before her, investigating the lines that cut deep through her skin.

"Julia." Charlie's voice was stern and coaxing.

Julia finally lifted her eyes toward his puppy-dog brown ones. How was it he could be exactly the same after all these years?

"What is it?"

"Happy birthday," he finally said, his eyes alight. He then reached forward, drawing his muscular arms around her and holding her tight against him. His embrace was warm, nourishing, and it made her anxious thoughts calm down. Very slowly, she returned to earth.

"I must smell terrible," Julia muttered into his shoulder.

"Me too," he said. "But I think we've smelled each other before."

Julia let out a laugh and sniffled and hiccupped all at once. Slightly embarrassed yet overwhelmed with emotion, she stepped back, took stock of him, and allowed herself to feel the depths of her emotions. Gosh, she'd loved him, and maybe she always would.

"Would you come to my birthday party later?" she asked timidly, feeling like a teenage girl asking a guy to the prom.

"You guys are having a classic Copperfield dinner?" Charlie asked.

"It just might be the very last one," Julia told him. "And I need you to be there, to help me say goodbye."

# Chapter Twenty-Nine

Back at The Copperfield House, a sweaty and grinning Julia entered through the back porch to discover the beautiful Greta Copperfield in a sea of French recipe books, all sat open across the countertops. Beside her, Rachel and Anna looked nervous yet attentive, with Rachel hovering over a skillet, a spatula poised, and Anna stirring up what looked to be the beginnings of cake batter. Carrot peelings were strewn across the floor, proof that one of her daughters was eager yet clumsy. Julia would take that any day of the week.

"Mom! Happy birthday!" Rachel cried joyously, nearly flinging the spatula to the ground.

"We've looked all over for you!" Anna said triumphantly, her spoon still whipping around the batter.

Still dressed in a satin robe, Greta rushed for Julia, her arms extended. She wrapped her third child in an embrace, bringing with her a wave of French perfume— the same that Alana had been wearing. "Happy birthday, darling. I love you so much. More today than yesterday."

"I love you, too. Are you wearing Alana's perfume?" Julia asked, laughing through the hug.

"Your sister has expensive taste," Greta returned as she stepped back. "She wants to train my nose. I told her that I'd already trained my nose enough with cooking. This got me thinking. When was the last time I had a proper French meal? It's not something I cooked up for myself over the years. And it's an appropriate way to say goodbye to this old place, isn't it?"

Julia blinked back tears and allowed her mother to explain her strategy for the meal ahead: fig and goat cheese tarts, duck breasts with cherry sauce, smoked salmon canapés, along with what would turn out to be a beautiful French-inspired carrot cake. Nobody had mentioned the duck à l'Orange incident since it had happened. Maybe they never would.

"It'll turn out if Anna here stirs a little bit faster," Greta affirmed, furrowing her brow.

"Doing my best, Grandma," Anna said, trying out the term "grandma" and smiling.

"I didn't spend a lot of time with them in the kitchen," Julia confessed to Greta sheepishly.

"I'll reprimand you for that another time," Greta told her. "We have a few hours until dinner. But in the meantime, I want you to hang around here with us while we cook. We've got wine chilling in the refrigerator, and Rachel reports that she has a music playlist that's perfect for cooking. You wanted a birthday. You've got a birthday."

Julia laughed outright, her stomach rumbling after the intensity of her workout.

"But darling, you really should shower first," Greta told her. "I hate to say this, but you stink."

Upstairs, Julia found Ella and Alana in the midst of an argument about when was best to move their mother into the new place in Manhattan. They were seated on Ella's teenage bed, staring straight ahead at Ella's previous collection of musical instruments, including a guitar that she'd carried around all through the nineties.

"I just think we should give her as much time as she needs to transition," Ella remarked.

"And I don't think it's going to matter. She'll drag her feet, regardless."

"Didn't you see the way Dad looked at Mom last night?" Ella asked. "Maybe it's too soon. Maybe we're pushing Quentin's agenda too far."

Julia rapped her knuckles against the doorframe. Alana and Ella turned their heads around, making the bed bounce beneath them.

"Happy birthday," they said in a bright, unison voice, although neither of them sounded particularly happy.

Julia stepped through and dropped to the floor, crossing her legs beneath her. "I need to tell you both about something."

Alana and Ella remained in rapt attention as Julia outlined her suspicions around Marcia Conrad, the emails, and their father's new manuscript, which was about a man who'd spent twenty-five years in prison for a crime he didn't commit.

"I think there's enough there to dispute the case," Julia told them.

"What about the statute of limitations?" Alana demanded.

"I don't know," Julia replied. "Maybe we can't put her in prison. But we could certainly smear her name through the mud and clear Dad's. Maybe that's all I really want, anyway. The concept of prison seems..." She shook her head ominously, searching for the right words. "It just seems insane to me to have to spend whole eras of your life locked away somewhere like a wild animal who can't be controlled. Aren't we humans? Aren't we capable of forgiveness?"

Alana and Ella considered this. They exchanged worried glances as though they half-suspected Julia was off her rocker.

"Just read the manuscript," Julia begged them. "I think you'll feel what I mean."

"I'll read it," Ella finally agreed. "But I still don't know if we should break our backs to try to clear Dad's name. Haven't we been through enough? Can't we just move forward?"

"The world thinks Dad is evil," Julia breathed. "But think about the man we knew back then. Think about the father he was and how much he loved our mother. Or about how he always asked us how we felt and what we wanted to be or how we wanted to live. And try to imagine that man doing the crime he did time for."

"That's been my struggle this entire time," Alana murmured, her eyes to the ground. "I couldn't picture our father being so cruel and manipulative. Not the man I'd always loved and respected."

"You don't have to decide anything right now," Julia breathed. "Just promise me that you'll think about it."

\* \* \*

Several hours later, dressed in a sleek black dress and a pair of tights, her hair styled and a bit of Alana's expensive perfume spritzed against her neck, Julia Copperfield sat at the head of the dining room table and watched as her beautiful mother, Greta, approached with a round carrot cake with cream cheese frosting. On the cake, she'd positioned seven candles (four decades plus three years equaled seven, according to Greta).

It was beyond Julia's wildest dreams.

Together, Greta, Alana, Ella, Rachel, Anna, Henry, and Charlie began to sing "Happy Birthday" to Julia, while Bernard stood off to the corner, his palms pressed together as his lips moved somberly. It wasn't clear if he made any sound at all. All that mattered was that he tried.

Greta placed the cake before Julia as the song finished up. Julia clenched her eyes tightly together and tried to come up with a perfect birthday wish, one that would eliminate all the pain from the past twenty-five years.

But all she could come up with was this:

*Please. Let us stay together this time.*

As the party-goers indulged in the decadent carrot cake, Julia stopped midway through her first slice to make an announcement. With her heart in her throat, she said, "The past few weeks have been some of the most visceral of my life. I was terrified to come back to The Copperfield House, terrified to see all of you again, and extremely terrified to face my own demons. It's all been beyond my wildest dreams. Surprisingly, I don't even mean that in a bad way."

Julia caught Charlie's eyes at this moment as her heart surged with hope for whatever it was they'd had and whatever it was they could build together.

"I recently learned that our father has been hard at work on another work of genius. He gave me the honor of reading it, which has allowed me a very emotional view into his world while in prison," Julia continued, her voice breaking with emotion. "I hope he doesn't mind that I read a small portion of his work this evening."

Julia locked eyes with her father, pleading with him wordlessly.

After a small and terrible pause, Bernard nodded.

"Before I begin," Julia continued, speeding up slightly due to embarrassment and excitement, "I'd like to say that my publishing house will be publishing Dad's work, hopefully with a release in late summer or early autumn. It will be an interesting process digging into this work with you, Dad. But I'm up for the challenge if you are. I should mention, too, that that will mean I'll be staying here at the house for a whole lot longer until we piece through the edits of the manuscript. And until I figure out what's next for me."

Julia searched through the pocket of her dress to find the folded-up sheet of paper she'd printed out earlier that afternoon. The print-out featured a particularly emotional portion of Bernard's novel, one she wished to translate to the rest of the family.

*There's a hollowness that comes from long days in prison. In the beginning of your sentence, your dreams trace all the memories you ever had— the birth of your first son, the first steps of your daughter, the laughter ringing out of your children's bedrooms as your wife tells them stories to help them go to sleep. But the dreams are a resource— and they become like the evaporating water at the bottom of a well. Very soon, your nights are just as hollow are your days, without reprieve from the aching horror of your inner mind.*

*What am I meant to do with all the love I still feel for the people who won't speak to me?*

*That's a funny thing, love. There's no evolutionary reason for humans to feel it, is there? And in my experience (especially given my current circumstances), I've never had a love that didn't end in complete disaster and heartache.*

*Yet still, I ask myself: how do I get through the hollowness of these long prison days?*

*And the answer, still— is love.*

*The memory of it, at least.*

*If I can find it within myself to hold on.*

As Julia read, tears welled in her eyes, making it difficult for her to make out the words. When she lifted her chin to gaze out across the dinner table, she found the rest of the Copperfield family, plus her children and Charlie, in similar states. No one spoke for a long time until Julia heard herself continue on.

"Look around you," Julia urged them. "There is so much

love here at this table. We abandoned it years ago, but we can get it back. If we work for it."

Silence welled over them. For a long moment, Julia thought for sure she'd overstepped her boundaries. *Who was she to plead with the family she'd abandoned to stay back, to rebuild with her? Who did she think she was?*

But suddenly, Bernard's textured baritone swelled across the table.

"Greta..." he began.

Greta turned her beautiful face toward his. She seemed captivated, the spitting image of the twenty-year-old woman she'd been when she met him in the streets of Paris.

"Greta, I know we can't get all that time back," he continued, his throat tightening. "But I'd like to ask you to give me a little more of it. Time, I mean. I don't deserve it. I don't deserve you. But you and I both know that I never really did."

"Bernard..." Greta whispered, her eyes welling with tears. "Bernard..." She splayed her hands over her eyes to avoid seeing any of them.

Beside her, Anna and Rachel clutched hands, their faces full of emotion.

There was no telling what would happen next.

Julia could only wait with bated breath.

When Greta removed her hands from her eyes, she gazed into Bernard's, her face glowing with forgiveness.

"My only dream for my life was to stay here with you for the rest of time," she told him, her voice shivering.

Beneath the table, Charlie placed a hand over Julia's.

"I don't know how much of ourselves we can get back," Greta whispered. "But how can I possibly run off to New York City when I have so much of my family right here with me?" She scowled as she added, "I've awoken to the terror of my wasted life. And I don't want to waste any more time. Especially not in some sterile community center in Manhattan. I'm not a city girl, anyway."

* * *

That night, Julia, Alana, and Ella sat out on the back porch of The Copperfield House and watched as the waves rolled toward them evenly, catching the soft light of the moon. Another slab of half-eaten cake rested between them on the back table, with much of its icing scraped off, and glasses of wine were strewn about. Julia had never been so sick to her stomach and so tired and so heartsick at once.

"So. Mom and Dad are...?" Alana began.

"I don't think they're back together," Ella affirmed. "I think they still love one another, but it's going to take time to heal."

"Well, at least they're not getting divorced. And they're not leaving. Not yet," Julia told them.

Ella puffed out her cheeks. "That passage you read in Dad's book..."

"It totally blew me away," Alana said.

Julia dropped her chin to her chest, listening to the rush of the waves and the sweep of the wind through the trees. How could she translate what the past few weeks had meant to her?

"You know, when Charlie left me in the city, I thought I was going to fall apart," Julia whispered. "I've felt ever since like I was just scrambling to tread water. A job here. A boyfriend there. Whoops! A kid. Then another and another. A mortgage and a bigger office and Botox and green smoothies."

Ella and Alana nodded knowingly.

"Being back on Nantucket has put together so many pieces of the puzzle for me," Julia continued. "I've been running away from my problems for too long. It's time to hunker down in this old place and really, truly breathe for the first time."

There on the back porch of The Copperfield house, Alana

and Ella wrapped their hands around Julia's as the three of them shared a beautiful silence, one pregnant with promise for the months ahead. They had no idea where the future would take them. But for the first time in twenty-five years, they knew they would take each step forward together, in love and in hope.

Coming Next in the Nantucket Sunset Series

Pre order Nantucket Dreams

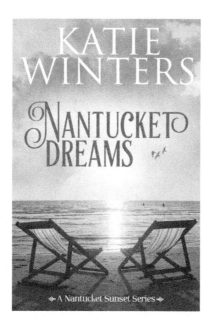